A JOKE A _

MY

FACEBOOK

2014

To Neil,

Happy Birthday!

Lorraine

Written by

Lorraine Tipene

PROFITS FROM THE SALE OF THIS BOOK
WILL GO TO THE NATIONAL AUTISTIC
SOCIETY GREAT BRITAIN

In support of

The National
Autistic Society

Registered as a charity
in England and Wales (269425)
and in Scotland (SC039427)

HEAVEN'S VERY SPECIAL CHILD

A meeting was held quite far from Earth!

It's time again for another birth.

Said the Angels to the LORD above,

This Special Child will need much love.

Her progress may be very slow,

Accomplishments she may not show.

And she'll require extra care

From the folks she meets down there.

She may not run or laugh or play,

Her thoughts may seem quite far away,

In many ways she won't adapt,

And she'll be known as handicapped.

So let's be careful where she's sent,

We want her life to be content.

Please LORD, find the parents who,

Will do a special job for you.

They will not realise right away

The leading role they're asked to play,

But with this child sent from above

Comes stronger faith and richer love.

And soon they'll know the privilege given

In caring for their gift from Heaven.

Their precious charge, so meek and mild,

IS HEAVEN'S VERY SPECIAL CHILD.

by Edna Massionilla

December 1981

What is Autism?

Autistic Spectrum Disorder, (ASD), is a complex condition where sufferers have difficulties in social interactions and communication. It is a lifelong developmental disability and most people diagnosed as having ASD have a normal life span. Unlike some other syndromes, most children classified as being autistic are perfectly normal in appearance, but spend their time engaged in puzzling, and sometimes disturbing behaviours which are noticeably different from those of typical children.

Recent studies have shown that approximately 9.6 per 10,000 children now have a diagnosis of ASD. ASD is about four times more common in boys than girls and the ratio of male to female diagnosis has remained consistent over the years. This gender difference is not unique to ASD, as many developmental disabilities have a greater male to female ratio. At least 75% of children diagnosed with ASD show signs of mental retardation. Females have lower IQ scores and also tend to have more severe symptoms and greater cognitive impairment.

The severity of the disorder varies dramatically between each child, and once diagnosed a child is placed somewhere on the autistic spectrum, falling in, or between, the categories of high functioning or low functioning ASD. ASD can be found throughout the world, in families of all racial, ethnic and social backgrounds, and no known factors in the psychological environment of a child have been shown to cause ASD.

Typical maladaptive behaviours include self injury, hand biting or head banging for example, aggression, hitting, spitting, and pushing, and destruction to property, whilst self-stimulatory behaviours include twirling objects, hand flapping, tapping, spinning, body rocking and masturbation. A major difficulty encountered by children diagnosed as autistic is that their characteristic self-stimulatory behaviour frequently interferes with on-task responding, positive social behaviours and learning.

To be diagnosed with autism, individuals must demonstrate a delay or abnormal functioning in either social interaction, language used for social communication or symbolic or imaginative play before the age of three, and demonstrate at least six of the following characteristics from all three of the main categories, with at least two from (A), and one each from (B) and (C):

Category A - Social interactions – manifested by:

1 – Failure to develop relationships with peers appropriate to developmental level.

2 – Marked impairment in the use of multiple non-verbal behaviours, eye to eye contact, facial expression, body postures and gestures.

3 – A lack of spontaneously seeking to share interests, showing enjoyment or achievements with other people.

4 – A lack of social or emotional reciprocity.

Category B – Communication – manifested by:

1 – A delay in, or total lack of, the development of spoken language.

2 – In individuals with adequate speech, the inability to initiate or sustain a conversation with other people.

3 – The lack of originality, and repetitive use of language, or idiosyncratic language.

4 – The lack of varied or spontaneous make-believe play, or imitative social play appropriate to developmental level.

Category 3 – Stereotypical behaviour – manifested by:

1 – Inflexible adherence to specific routines or rituals.

2 – A comprehensive preoccupation with one or more stereotyped and restricted patterns of interest that is abnormal either in focus or intensity.

3 – Stereotyped and repetitive motor mannerisms - hand or finger flapping, rocking or complex whole body movements, for example.

4 – Persistent preoccupation with an object or parts of an object.

A typical autistic child's behaviour is likely to include:

- no speech
- non-speech vocalizations: repeating a sound over and over
- delayed speech development

- echolalia: repeating something said to them
- delayed echolalia: repeating something heard at an earlier time
- confusion between the pronouns "I" and "You"
- lack of interaction with other children and adults
- lack of eye to eye contact
- lack of response to people
- inappropriate behaviour: no sense of modesty, over familiarity
- offering no help when picked up (feels like lifting a sack of potatoes)
- preoccupation with hands or other body part
- an extended interest in moving objects
- self-stimulatory, repetitive, behaviour: flapping hands, spinning, rocking
- balancing: walking along a low beam, walking on tiptoes
- a preference to pull a person by the hand to show them an object rather than speak

- extreme dislike of certain sounds, putting fingers in ears to block out sounds
- extreme dislike of touching certain textures
- dislike of being touched
- hyperactivity or hypo-activity
- extreme dislike of certain foods, drinking and/or eating the same food items at every meal
- behaviour that is aggressive to others
- lack of interest in toys
- lack of make-believe play
- desire to follow set patterns of behaviour/interaction, insistence of sameness
- desire to keep objects in a certain physical pattern: order of books, videos etc.
- self-injury: hand biting, head banging
- normal or advanced competence: mathematics, memory, drawing and musical skills.

(American Psychiatric Association, 2000)

New Year's Eve 2013

I was reading all the posts wishing everyone a Happy New Year etc, when I came up with my own post. This is what it said.

"OK, everyone always wishes everyone else a Happy New Year so my contribution to making your 2014 a very happy year is to endeavour to tell you a new joke every day starting with this one:

It was that time, during the Sunday morning service, for the children's sermon.

All the children were invited to come forward.

One little girl was wearing a particularly pretty dress and, as she sat down, the minister leaned over and said, 'That is a very pretty dress. Is it your Easter Dress?'

The little girl replied, directly into the minister's clip-on microphone, 'Yes and my Mum said it's a bitch to iron.'

At the beginning that was all I intended to do, but as the year wore on people were asking me to continue the joke telling into 2015 and telling me how much the joke of the day meant to them. Some people were messaging me to ask if I was ok if I was a bit late posting my joke, others told me it brightened their day and it was the first thing they did when they logged into facebook. Others thanked me and shared my jokes. This got me thinking that if everyone was enjoying them, why not share them in a book and raise funds for a deserving cause at the same time?

The National Autistic Society UK has been my chosen charity because my daughter Rachel is autistic. The NAS (UK) is the leading charity for people with autism, including Asperger Syndrome and their families. Around 700,000 people in the UK have autism. Together with their families they make up over 2.7 million people whose lives are touched by autism every single day. Nothing can prepare you for the changes your life takes when you get the autism diagnosis, it affects every member of the family in a different way. Families need support not just from each other but from outside sources as well. From good times to challenging times, The National Autistic Society is there at every stage, to help transform the lives of everyone living with autism.

With nearly 50 years of experience in developing and providing innovative and pioneering services, the NAS can give children with autism the very best start in life, and they will continue to learn, innovate and share good practice. The NAS also provide a lifeline for many hundreds of families who need support to care for their loved ones.

They have nearly 20,000 members, around 100 branches and provide:

- information, advice, advocacy, training and support for individuals and their families
- information and training for health, education and other professionals working with people with autism and their families
- specialist residential, supported living, outreach and day services for adults
- specialist schools and education outreach services for children
- out-of-school services for children and young people
- employment training and support and social programmes for adults with autism.

The money raised from the sale of this book will help the NAS to help people with autism and their families, and help to provide information, support and pioneering services, and campaign for a better world for people with autism.

   I hope you enjoy the jokes in this book as much as my facebook friends did. I don't know the origin of them, some were told to me over the years, others emailed to me and some I found on the world wide web.

You might be an autism parent if..........

There is a great twitter page called youmightbeanautismparentif.

 Many parents of autistic children send tweets in and I have placed a few that we can relate to throughout the book to share stories with you about Rachel. If you are an 'autism parent' then you will probably also relate to a lot of the tweets and if you are not an 'autism parent' it will give you an understanding into the daily lives of those on the spectrum and their families. (Please remember Rachel is 25years old and this is day to day happenings that we are still living with).

This book has been made possible by the generosity of the following people through a crowd funding initiative. I have been totally overwhelmed with people's generosity and I thank each and every one of you from the bottom of my heart. I think you are all amazing!

John Downton and Katia Gershun

Sophie Jane Evans

Nigel and Leo Forshaw

Darren Campbell

Carolyn and Barrie Smith

Lucy Lu

David and Sharon Irvine

Emma and Richard Lee

Craig Tipene and Naomi Campbell

Susan Hands

Carole, Jason and Jacqueline Sampson Joseph

Joan Nicholson and Keith Makin

Sandra and Tony Lawrence

Peter Jones and MUFC

Bernie and Brian Nicholson

Joanne Littlewood

Liz Hemmings

Alexandra Mowatt and Dan Shakespeare

Howard and Margaret Greene

Tony and Heather Brewster

Tracey and Nigel Gooding

Carole and Fred Jolly

Eimear Fitzgerald

Patricia Greenwood

Carol Robinson

Tony and Jill Rothwell

Patricia Hamilton

Caroline Stirling

Sue Pierson

Shaun Thompson

Penny Gasparini

Maria and Ian Roberts

Gary Leighton

Debbie Byrne

Ann-Marie Whurr

Kay Bartenschlager

Lucy Coote

RACHEL'S STORY

A lot of mothers, when asked if they want a boy or a girl when they are pregnant, will reply with "It doesn't matter as long as it has ten fingers and ten toes" while secretly hoping for a perfect baby with rosebud lips who sleeps through the night and has no trouble feeding. Every mother wants a baby that will roll over, sit up and take those first steps right on schedule. Every mother wants a baby that can see, hear, run, jump and speak. A child who will have loads of friends throughout school and gets invited to friend's birthday parties. Who grows up and follows their dreams – a job, marries, has a family of their own and travels the world. Most of all, a child who has their independence.

What happens when you don't get that PERFECT baby? What happens when you get a whole lot more...

People always ask me if I knew from the beginning that Rachel was autistic. The answer to that is 'No' but as I already had one child, Craig, I knew things were not 'right' with her. She was born at 3pm on the 15th of February 1990 in England. It was a full term pregnancy with no birthing complications. Her birth weight at 5lbs 11oz was 4oz heavier than her brother Craig had been four years previous. The midwife said "Small Mum, small baby," as she weighed her, before handing the screaming little bundle to me. Rachel felt different. Her skin was too large for her tiny body and hung off her, she had no muscle tone whatsoever, and her ears were folded down at the tops. She would tire quickly when she had her bottle, never finishing it, and she failed to thrive.

For the first three months of her life she couldn't focus her eyes and would constantly move them from side to side. Fearing that she was blind, we visited a hospital consultant who suggested she had hydrocephalus as her head was growing rapidly. They sent her for scans which showed the ventricles in her brain were enlarged, a sign that she had increased fluid in her brain, and we talked about the possibility of her having to have a cerebral shunt fitted to bypass the obstruction and relieve it. We used to dread going to the hospital every two weeks, and I remember sitting in the waiting room repeating in my head, "Please don't let her head have grown", even though I knew through my own measurements that it had.

One morning after three months had gone by, I was getting Rachel dressed when I noticed that she was looking at me. Her eyes had stopped moving from side to side and she was really content and smiling. The water which was causing pressure on her brain had found its own release and at last I had my happy little girl. It also meant that she didn't need an operation to fit a cerebral shunt. The relief I felt was enormous and I naively thought that everything would be fine from there on out. Unfortunately it was just the beginning of a very long road for us.

From birth I noticed Rachel had talipes (a club foot) which affected her right foot, and I believe that if Rachel didn't have this she may have been overlooked somewhat with the treatment she received further down the line. We had a great physiotherapist called Helen who came to our house three times a week to strap Rachel's foot and teach me how to do the stretching exercises to help straighten it. I could talk to her about the fears I had about Rachel, especially when she wasn't reaching her baby milestones.

When Rachel was eight months old Helen told me she thought Rachel had cerebral palsy. She still wasn't thriving and could not eat any solid foods from a spoon.

She was so small, bodily, that she was still wearing clothes for a three month old, although her head was the size of a two year old. She was a very floppy baby with very low muscle tone. At that time she could not hold her head up or roll over from her back onto her tummy etc, which are all milestones for a five month old baby, let alone sit up either with support or independently, which a six month old baby is usually capable of. Thankfully my brother had sent a special baby sheepskin rug over from New Zealand, where he was living at the time, for her to lie on and that was how she viewed the world for many months, lying flat on her back on the living room carpet.

Helen suggested that Rachel would benefit from attending the STAR Centre in St Helens, which is a unit for children with special needs where they can access various services all under one roof. A physiotherapist, speech therapist, occupational therapist etc, would see Rachel on a Monday morning and the consultant would also come along every couple of months to save us the slog of going to the hospital. It was a brilliant setup and it also gave the parents a chance to talk.

Helen gave me lots of exercises to do with Rachel to strengthen her neck muscles so she would be able to hold her head up and roll over from front to back. I did them all religiously at every nappy change because Helen told me that the more you do the exercises, the sooner the brain remembers the movements. By the time Rachel was given a place at the STAR Centre at eleven months old, she could hold her head up for short periods but was still unable to sit independently. The STAR Centre ordered a special seat which had a padded post between her legs to stop her sliding down, a wide Velcro strap which went around her chest to hold her upright and a small desk so that she could play with her toys.

At twelve months old she weighed 15lbs and was wearing clothes for a three to six month old baby. She got her first pair of boots, white orthopaedic ones that looked bigger than her legs, and a few weeks later a wooden standing frame was delivered. It was a large contraption which was tilted forward slightly to help her remain upright. It changed her perspective on the world. Now, she could see it from higher up instead of from the floor, and from then she came on in leaps and bounds.

Over the next 12 months she started to eat solid foods and gained weight. She learnt to sit independently, roll over and then to commando crawl around the room.

She would stand in front of the television in her standing frame and flap her arms to the music. She was always happy and always smiling but she wasn't verbal.

She had speech therapy every week, blowing bubbles, sipping drinks through straws, licking her lips etc, all designed to make her more aware of her mouth and tongue. She didn't babble like other babies and we started to use Makaton sign language to communicate. I would sit with her and Craig and we would say and sign the pictures. Craig was only five or six at this time and he was fantastic. He also learned to sign and he would read books and sing and sign nursery rhymes to her. We did puzzles; wooden picture puzzles and computer based ones on a computer that the STAR Centre provided for her with a touch screen, colouring in, ball rolling and parachute play to help cognitive and motor skills. We also did water and sand play to develop sensory skills, and lots of book reading and singing. Lots and lots of singing!

The physiotherapist had warned me that because all her ligaments are soft and she is loose jointed, she would probably never walk. I refused to believe this diagnosis and set about walking Rachel up and down the road, her legs splaying out unevenly and wobbling like a drunk several times a day. She was also given a walking frame which she soon learnt to propel around the house, and she surprised everyone when she started walking at the age of two. For the first couple of years after she found her feet we shepherded her like a new born lamb because she had no saving reflex and each time she lost her balance she would invariably fall flat on her face. I lost count of the number of split lips she received.

At five years old she was finally nappy free during the day, and she started school part time at the Hurst School for children with special educational needs in the language unit. Rachel was quite mobile by this time but still unsteady on her feet, and she came home every day with plasters on her knees from falling over in the playground. The teacher was so concerned that we bought some knee pads used by skateboarders for them to put on her during playtime.

It was around this time that we suspected Rachel might be autistic although when I questioned her paediatrician she dismissed it as Rachel just being lazy. She had shown such determination in her ability to learn to walk and feed and use a cup that I knew deep down in my heart she was wrong.

We asked to see an educational psychologist to get a diagnosis and within five minutes of walking into her office she agreed with us.

"Yes, Rachel is autistic."

We still had to go through the motions and sit through three hours of questions before we got the 'paperwork' and nothing changed. She wasn't treated any differently, it was just a label.

Like a lot of families, having an autistic member of the family has had a profound positive impact on our perceptions and expectations. Our lives have been enriched and enhanced in so many ways. We are more tolerant towards other people. We have more patience. Things that once we would have rushed are taken at a slower pace and things that would have upset us before are brushed to one side. The small things don't matter anymore.

We are fortunate to have a very, *very* happy daughter. She brings laughter and smiles to everyone she meets. Her innocence and childlike behaviour is her redeeming feature. Bear this in mind when reading about her, she isn't naughty and despite being 25 years old she is just like a three year old child in a lot of ways. She doesn't know the consequences of her actions and she doesn't know the rules of life. Personal space and modesty are alien to her. Rachel is a law unto herself.

It would be wrong to portray a picture of perfect happiness and our lives are ruled by her, 24 hours a day, 7 days a week.

Autism isn't the end of the world. It's the beginning of a whole new one.

January

January 1st

A drunken man who smelled like beer sat down on a subway next to a priest.

The man's tie was stained; his face was plastered with red lipstick and a half empty bottle of gin was sticking out of his torn coat pocket

He opened his newspaper and began reading.

After a few minutes the man turned to the priest and asked, 'Say Father, what causes arthritis?'

The priest, wanting to teach this man a little lesson replied, 'My son, it's caused by loose living, being with cheap, wicked women, too much alcohol, contempt for your fellow man, sleeping around with prostitutes and lack of a bath.'

The drunk muttered in response, 'Well, I'll be damned,' then returned to his paper.

The priest, thinking about what he had said, nudged the man and apologised. 'I'm very sorry. I didn't mean to come on so strong. How long have you had arthritis?'

The drunk answered, 'I don't have it, Father. I was just reading here that the Pope does.

January 2nd

An Irishman goes to the Doctor with bottom problems....

'Doctor, it's me ahrse. I'd loik ya ta take a look, if ya would'.

So the doctor gets him to drop his pants and takes a look.

'Incredible' he says, 'there is a £20 note lodged up here.'

Tentatively he eases the twenty out of the man's bottom, and then a £10 pound note appears.

'This is amazing!' exclaims the Doctor. ''What do you want me to do?'

'Well for goodness sake take it out, man! Shrieks the patient.
The doctor pulls out the tenner and another twenty appears, and another and another and another and another and another and so it went on.
Finally the last note comes out and no more appears.
'Ah Doctor, tank ya koindly, dat's much better. Just out of interest, how much was in there then?'
The Doctor counts the pile of cash and says '£1,990 exactly.'
'Ah, dat'd be roit," says the Irishman,
'Ah knew Ah wasn't feeling two grand.

January 3rd

A guy gets shipwrecked and, when he wakes up, he's on a beach.
 The sand is dark red. He can't believe it.
 The sky is dark red.
He walks around a bit and sees there is dark red grass, dark red birds and dark red fruit on the dark red trees.
 He's shocked when he finds that his skin is starting to turn dark red too.
"Oh no!" he says. "I think that I've been marooned!"

Comments on this particular post read like this:
"terrible"
"Might be terrible but it makes us laugh each morning!!!
Thx and keep it up Lorraine" xx
"You are keeping this up for a year!!?"
And "It's awful but I love it!"

☺☺

January 4th

A man with a winking problem is applying for a position as a sales representative for a large firm.

The interviewer looks over his papers and says. "This is phenomenal; you've graduated from the best schools, your recommendations are wonderful, and your experience is unparalleled. Normally, we'd hire you without a second thought. However, a sales representative has a highly visible position and we're afraid that your constant winking will scare off potential customers".

"Hang on," the man says. "All I need to do is take two aspirins, they stop me winking!"...

"Really" says the interviewer? "Great! Show me!"

So the applicant reaches into his jacket pocket and begins pulling out all sorts of condoms: red condoms, blue condoms, ribbed condoms, flavoured condoms; finally, at the bottom, he finds a packet of aspirin. He tears it open, swallows the pills, and stops winking.

"Well," said the interviewer, "that's all well and good, but this is a respectable company, and we will not have our employees womanizing all over the country."

"Womanizing? What do you mean? I'm a happily married man!"

"Well then, how do you explain all these condoms?"

"Oh, that," he sighed. "Have you ever walked into a pharmacy, winking, and asked for aspirin?"

January 5th

A man who just died is delivered to a Glasgow mortuary wearing an expensive, expertly tailored black suit. Big Tam the mortician asks the deceased's wife how she would like the body dressed.

He points out that the man does look very good in the black suit he is already wearing.

The widow, however, says that she always thought her husband looked his best in blue.

She gives Tam a blank cheque and says, "I don't care what it costs, but please have my husband in a blue suit for the viewing."

The woman returns the next day and to her delight she finds her husband dressed in a gorgeous blue suit with a subtle chalk stripe; the suit fits him perfectly.

She says to Tam, "Whatever the cost, I'm very satisfied. You did an excellent job and I'm very grateful. How much did you spend?"

To her astonishment, Tam presents her with the blank cheque.

"Nae charge", he says.

"No, really, I must pay you for the cost of that exquisite blue suit!" she says.

"Honestly, hen", Tam says, "it didnae cost nothin. You see, a dead gentleman of about your husband's size was brought in shortly after you left yesterday, and he was wearing an attractive blue suit.

I asked his missus if she minded him going to his grave wearing a black suit instead, and she said it made nae difference as long as he looked nice."

"So, I just switched their heads."

January 6th
An employer has an Irishman apply for a job and as he doesn't really want to employ him, he decides to set a

puzzle for him on the assumption that he won't be able to answer and then he can justify not giving him the job. He tells the Irishman that he is not allowed to use numbers or letters but he wants him to show him the number nine.
The Irishman thinks for a bit then gets a piece of paper and draws 3 trees on it. The employer says "What´s that?"
The Irishman says "Tree trees are noin (nine)"
The employer thinks that was too easy so he tells the Irishman to do the same thing with the number 99.
The Irishman takes the picture of the three trees and rubs his fingers over the drawing, smudging it badly. "Der you go - dat´s 99"
"What?" says the employer "How´s that 99?"
The Irishman replies "Dirty tree, dirty tree and dirty tree makes 99!"
The employers thinks to himself that the Irishman´s smarter than he looks so he decides to make the last one impossible and tells the Irishman to do the same thing again but this time making a total of 100.
The Irishman thinks for ages and the employer´s just about to get rid of him when he says "Oi´ve got it! The Irishman takes the picture of the three dirty trees and draws a small circle at the side of each tree - "Dat´s it den - 100!"
The employer´s really puzzled and says "I finally got the other two but how on earth does that represent 100?
 The Irishman says "It´s easy - dirty tree and a turd, dirty tree and a turd, dirty tree and a turd!"

January 7th
Anyone who lived in England at this time was reminded every day about the so called influx of immigrants due to

hit our shores from Bulgaria and Romania. So a quick joke was the order of the day.

It's the 7th of January and I haven't seen one Bulgarian yet.

I've only been in Bulgaria 5 days though.

Strange thing is though one of my friends comments made people laugh even more.

Quote "Didn't know you were going away - enjoy xxx" (the mind boggles)

January 8th

A tourist in Vienna is going through a graveyard and all of a sudden he hears music. No one is around, so he starts searching for the source.

He finally locates the origin and finds it is coming from a grave with a headstone that reads: "Ludwig van Beethoven, 1770- 1827". Then he realizes that the music is Beethoven's Ninth Symphony and it is being played backward!

Puzzled, he leaves the graveyard and persuades a friend to return with him.

By the time they arrive back at the grave, the music has changed. This time it is the Seventh Symphony, but like the previous piece, it is being played backwards. Curious, the men agree to consult a music scholar.

When they return with the expert, the Fifth Symphony is playing, again backwards.

The expert notices that the symphonies are being played in the reverse order to which they were composed, the 9th, then the 7th, then the 5th.

By the next day the word had spread, and a crowd has gathered around the grave. They are all listening to the Second Symphony being played backward.
 Just then the graveyard's caretaker ambles up to the group.
Someone in the group asks him if he has an explanation for the music.
"I would have thought it was obvious," the caretaker says. "He's decomposing."

January 9th
A married couple were driving at 55MPH the wife behind the wheel.
 Her husband says "Honey I know we have been married for 15 years but I want a divorce"
The wife says nothing and accelerates to 60MPH.
 He then says "I don't want you to talk me out of it I'm having an affair with your best friend and she is prettier than you"
 The wife says nothing and accelerates.
 "I want the house" he says.
Again the wife accelerates to 70MPH.
 "I want the kids too" he says.
The wife keeps going faster and faster passing 80MPH.
 "Is there nothing you want" he says as they approach the bridge.
 "No I've got everything I need"
 "What's that?" He asks.
 She says just before they hit the wall "I've got the airbag"

January 10th

Martha recently lost her husband. She had him cremated and brought his ashes home.

Picking up the urn that he was in, she poured him out on the patio table.

Then, while tracing her fingers in the ashes, she started talking to him....

"You know that dishwasher you promised me? I bought it with the insurance money!"

She paused for a minute tracing her fingers in the ashes then said,

"Remember that car you promised me? Well, I also bought it with the insurance money!"

Again, she paused for a few minutes and while tracing her fingers in the ashes she said,

"Remember that diamond ring you promised me? I bought it too, with the insurance money!"

Finally, still tracing her fingers in the ashes, she said,

"Remember that blow job I promised you? Here it comes!"

January 11th

Two Men are out fishing when one decides to have a smoke.

He asks his friend if he has a lighter.

'Sure', he replies and hands over a 10 inch long BIC lighter.

Surprised the guy says, "That's quite a lighter! Where did you get it?'

'Oh, I have a personal genie, gives me anything I want.'

Incredulous, the first man asks 'Can I make a wish? '

'Sure, just make sure that you speak clearly because he is a little hard of hearing'

'OK I will', says the other, and as he rubs the lamp, sure enough, a genie appears and asks the man what he wants
The man yells. 'I want a Million Bucks'
The genie says OK and goes back in his lamp and 10 seconds later a million ducks fly overhead.
Disappointed, the guy says 'Your genie certainly does have problem hearing doesn't he?'
The other man says, 'I know, do you really think I asked for a 10 inch BIC?'

January 12th

Three old mischievous Grandmas were sitting on a bench outside a nursing home.
About then an old Grandpa walked by, and one of the old Grandma's yelled out saying,
'We bet we can tell exactly how old you are.'
The old man said, 'There ain't no way you can guess it, you old fools.'
One of the old Grandmas said, 'Sure we can! Just drop your pants and under shorts and we can tell your exact age.'
Embarrassed just a little, but anxious to prove they couldn't do it, he dropped his drawers.
The Grandmas asked him to first turn around a couple of times and to jump up and down several times.
Then they all piped up and said, 'You're 87 years old!'
Standing with his pants down around his ankles, the old gent asked, 'How in the world did you guess?'
Slapping their knees and grinning from ear to ear, all three old ladies happily yelled in unison--
'We were at your birthday party yesterday!'

January 13th

Paddy's pregnant sister was in a terrible car accident and went into a deep coma. After being in the coma for nearly six months, she wakes up and sees that she is no longer pregnant. Frantically, she asks the doctor about her baby. The doctor replies, 'Ma'am, you had twins.... a boy and a girl. The babies are fine, however, they were poorly at birth and had to be christened immediately so your brother Paddy came in and named them.
The woman thinks to herself, ' Oh suffering Jaysus, no, not me brother, he's a bloody clueless idiot...
Expecting the worst, she asks the doctor,' well, what's my daughter's name?'
'Denise' says the doctor.
The new mother is somewhat relieved, 'Wow, that's a beautiful name, I guess I was wrong about my brother', she thought....'I really like Denise'
Then she asks, ' What's the boy's name?'
The doctor replies ' Denephew'

January 14th

What is the difference between erotic and kinky?
Erotic is where you use a feather, kinky you use the whole chicken........

January 15th

Three sisters, ages 92, 94, and 96, live in a house together.

One night the 96-year-old draws a bath, puts her foot in and pauses. She yells down the stairs, "Was I getting in or out of the bath?"

The 94-year-old yells back, "I don't know. I'll come up and see." She starts up the stairs and pauses. "Was I going up the stairs or down?"

The 92-year-old is sitting at the kitchen table having tea listening to her sisters. She shakes her head and says, "I hope I never get that forgetful" and knocks on wood for good measure.

She then yells, "I'll come up and help both of you as soon as I see who's at the door.

January 16th

A Bloke's wife goes missing while diving off the West Australian coast. He reports the event, searches fruitlessly and spends a terrible night wondering what could have happened to her.

Next morning there's a knock at the door and he is confronted by a couple of policemen, the old Sergeant and a younger Constable.

The Seargent says, 'Mate, we have some news for you. Unfortunately, some really bad news, some good news, and maybe some more good news'.

'Well,' says the bloke, 'I guess I'd better have the bad news first?'

The Sergeant says, 'I'm really sorry mate, but your wife is dead. Young Bill here found her lying at about five fathoms in a little cleft in the reef. He got a line around her and we pulled her up, but she was dead.'

The bloke is naturally pretty distressed to hear of this, but after a few minutes he pulls himself together and asks what the good news is.

The Sergeant says, 'Well when we got your wife up there were quite a few really good sized crayfish and a swag of nice crabs attached to her, so we've brought you your share.'

He hands the bloke a big sugar bag with a couple of nice crayfish and four or five crabs in it.

'Geez thanks. They're bloody beauties! So what's the other possible good news?'

'Well', the Sergeant says, 'if you fancy a quick trip, me and young Bill here get off duty at around 11 o'clock and we're gonna shoot over there and pull her up again!'

January 17th

One evening a Husband, thinking he was being funny, said to his wife, 'Perhaps we should start washing your clothes in 'Slim Fast'. Maybe it would take a few inches off of your butt!'

His wife was not amused, and decided that she simply couldn't let such a comment go unrewarded.

The next morning the husband took a pair of underwear out of his drawer. 'What the Hell is this?' he said to himself as a little 'dust' cloud appeared when he shook them out.

'April', he hollered into the bathroom, 'Why did you put talcum pplowder in my underwear?'

She replied with a snicker, 'It's not talcum powder; it's 'Miracle Grow'!!!!!

January 18th

A man boarded an aircraft at London's Heathrow Airport for New York, and taking his seat as he settled in, he noticed a very beautiful woman boarding the plane. He realised she was heading straight toward his seat and bingo - she took the seat right beside him.

"Hello", he blurted out, "Business trip or vacation?"

She turned, smiled enchantingly and said, "Business. I'm going to the
annual nymphomaniac convention in the United States."

He swallowed hard. Here was the most gorgeous woman he had ever seen sitting next to him, and she was going to a meeting for nymphomaniacs!

Struggling to maintain his composure, he calmly asked, "What's your business role at this convention?"

"Lecturer," she responded." I use my experience to debunk some of the popular myths about sexuality."

"Really", he smiled, "what myths are those?"

"Well," she explained, "one popular myth is that African-American men are the most well-endowed when, in fact, it's the Native American Indian who is most likely to possess that trait. Another popular myth is that French men are the best lovers, when actually it is the men of Greek descent. We have also found that the best potential lovers in all categories are the Irish."

Suddenly the woman became uncomfortable and blushed. "I'm sorry," she said. "I really shouldn't be discussing this with you; I don't even know your name!"

"Tonto," the man said. "Tonto Papadopoulos, but my friends call me Paddy".

☺☺

January 19th

One afternoon a Scotsman was riding in his limousine when he saw two men along the roadside eating grass. Disturbed, he ordered his driver to stop and he got out to investigate.

He asked one man, "Why are you eating grass?"

"We don't have any money for food," the poor man replied. "We have to eat grass."

"Well, then, you can come with me to my house and I'll feed you," the Scotsman said.

"But sir, I have a wife and two children with me. They are over there, under that tree."

"Bring them along," the Scotsman replied.

Turning to the other poor man he stated, "You come with us, also."

The second man, in a pitiful voice, then said, "But sir, I also have a wife and SIX children with me!"

"Bring them all, as well," the Scotsman answered.

They all entered the car, which was no easy task, even for a car as large as the limousine was.

Once under way, one of the poor fellows turned to the Scotsman and said, "Sir, you are too kind. Thank you for taking all of us with you."

The Scotsman replied, "Glad to do it. You'll really love my place. The grass is almost a foot high."

January 20th

Fred came home drunk one night, slid into bed beside his sleeping wife, and fell into a deep slumber.

He awoke before the Pearly Gates, where St. Peter said, 'You died in your sleep, Fred.'

Fred was stunned. 'I'm dead?

No, I can't be! I've got too much to live for. Send me back!'
St. Peter said, 'I'm sorry, but there's only one way you can
go back, and that is as a chicken.'
Fred was devastated, but begged St. Peter to send him to
a farm near his home.
The next thing he knew, he was covered with feathers,
clucking and pecking the ground.
A rooster strolled past. 'So, you're the new hen, huh?
How's your first day here?'
'Not bad,' replied Fred the hen, 'but I have this strange
feeling inside. Like I'm gonna explode!'
'You're ovulating,' explained the rooster. 'Don't tell me
you've never laid an egg before?'
'Never,' said Fred.
'Well, just relax and let it happen,' says the rooster. 'It's no
big deal.'
He did, and a few uncomfortable seconds later, out
popped an egg! He was overcome with emotion as he
experienced motherhood. He soon laid another egg -- his
joy was overwhelming.
As he was about to lay his third egg, he felt a smack on the
back of his head, and heard.....
"Fred, wake up! You've pooed in the bed!"

January 21ˢᵗ

"Can I have some Irish Sausages, please?" asked the
Irishman, walking up to the counter.
The assistant looked at him and asked: "Are you Irish?"
"If I had asked you for Italian sausage, would you ask me if
I was Italian?" demanded the Irishman indignantly. "Or, if I
asked for German Bratwurst, would you ask me if I was
German?"

Then, warming to his theme, he went on: "Or if I asked you for a Kosher hot dog, would you ask me if I was Jewish?"
"Or, if I asked you for a taco, would you ask me if I was Mexican?! Would Ya? Would Ya?"
The assistant said: "Well, no."
Suitably encouraged by the success of his logic, the Irishman steps it up a gear.
"And if I asked you for frogs legs, would you ask me if I was French?"
"What about Danish Bacon, would you ask me if I was Danish?"
"Well no, I probably wouldn't" conceded the assistant.
So, now bursting with righteous indignation, the Irishman says: "Well, all right then, why did you ask me if I'm Irish just because I asked for Irish sausages?"
The assistant replied: "Because you're in bloody Homebase"

January 22nd
Bob walked into a sports bar around 9:58 PM.
He sat down next to a blonde at the bar and stared up at the TV. The 10 PM news was coming on and the news crew was covering the story of a man on the ledge of a large building preparing to jump.
The blonde looked at Bob and said, "Do you think he'll jump?"
Bob said, "You know, I bet he'll jump."
The blonde replied, "Well, I bet he won't."
Bob placed a $20 bill on the bar and said, "You're on!"
Just as the blonde placed her money on the bar, the guy on the ledge did a swan dive off the building, falling to his death.

The blonde was very upset, but willingly handed her $20 to Bob.

"Fair's fair. Here's your money."

Bob replied, "I can't take your money. I saw this earlier on the 5 PM news, so I knew he would jump."

The blonde replied, "I did, too, but I didn't think he'd do it again."

January 23rd

Three Hillbillies are sitting on a porch shootin' the breeze.

1st Hillbilly says: 'My wife sure is stupid! She bought an air conditioner.'

2nd Hillbilly says: 'Why is that stupid?'

1st Hillbilly says: 'We ain't got no 'lectricity!'

2nd Hillbilly says: 'That's nothin'! My wife is so stupid; she bought one of them new-fangled warshin' machines!'

1st Hillbilly says: 'Why is that so stupid?'

2nd Hillbilly says: ''Cause we ain't got no plummin'!'

3rd Hillbilly says: 'That ain't nuthin'! My wife is dumber than both yer wives put together! I was going through her purse the other day lookin' fer some change, and I found 6 condoms in thar.'

1st and 2nd Hillbillies say: 'Well, what's so dumb about that?'

3rd Hillbilly says: 'She ain't got no dick!'

January 24th

Every day, a male co-worker walks up very close to a lady standing at the coffee machine, inhales a big breath of air and tells her that her hair smells nice.

After a week of this, she can't stand it anymore, and takes her complaint to a supervisor in the personnel department and states that she wants to write a sexual harassment grievance against him.

The Human Resources supervisor is puzzled by this decision and asks, "What's sexually threatening about a co-worker telling you your hair smells nice?"

The woman replies, "It's Keith, the dwarf."

January 25th

There is a factory in Essex which makes the Tickle Me Elmo toys. The toy laughs when you tickle it under the arms. Well, Shelly is hired at The Tickle Me Elmo factory and she reports for her first day promptly at 8:00 am.

The next day at 8:45 am there is a knock at the Personnel Manager's door. The Foreman throws open the door and begins to rant about the new employee. He complains that she is incredibly slow and the whole line is backing up, putting the entire production line behind schedule.

The Personnel Manager decides he should see this for himself, so the 2 men march down to the factory floor.

When they get there the line is so backed up that there are Tickle Me Elmo's all over the factory floor and they're really beginning to pile up.

At the end of the line stands Shelly surrounded by mountains of Tickle Me Elmo's. She has a roll of plush Red fabric and a huge bag of small marbles.

The 2 men watch in amazement as she cuts a little piece of fabric, wraps it around two marbles and begins to carefully sew the little package between Elmo's legs. The Personnel Manager bursts into laughter. After several minutes of hysterics he pulls himself together and approaches Shelly. 'I'm sorry,' he says to her, barely able to keep a straight face, 'but I think you misunderstood the instructions I gave you yesterday...'

"Your job is to give Elmo two test tickles."

January 26th

Bill and his blonde wife Bambi live in Cheyenne. One winter morning while listening to the radio, they hear the announcer say, "We are going to have 3 to 4 inches of snow today. You must park your car on the even-numbered side of the street, so the snowplough can get through."

Bambi goes out and moves her car to the appropriate side of the street.

A week later while they are eating breakfast, the radio announcer says, "We are expecting 4 to 5 inches of snow today. You must park your car on the odd numbered side of the street so the snowplough can get through."

Again, Bambi goes out and moves her car to the designated location.

The next week they are having breakfast again, when the radio announcer says "We are expecting 10 to 12 inches of snow today. You must park....." and then the electricity goes out.

Bambi says, "Honey, I don't know what to do."

Bill says, "Why don't you just leave the car in the garage this time?"

☺☺

January 27th

An RAF Airman pulled into a little town, and found every hotel room was taken.

"You've got to have a room somewhere," he pleaded. "Or just a bed, I don't care where."

"Well, I do have a double room with one occupant, a Royal Marine guy," admitted the manager, "and he might be glad to split the cost. But to tell you the truth, he snores so loudly that people in adjoining rooms have complained in the past. I'm not sure it'd be worth it to you."

"No problem," the tired Airman assured him. "I'll take it."

The next morning the Airman came down to breakfast bright-eyed and bushy-tailed.

"How'd you sleep?" asked the manager.

"I've never slept better."

The manager was impressed. "No problem with the other guy snoring, then?"

"Nope, I shut him up in no time." said the Airman.

"How'd you manage that?" asked the manager.

"He was already in bed, snoring away, when I came in the room," the Airman explained.

"I went over, gave him a kiss on the cheek, said, 'Goodnight, sweetie!' and he sat up all night watching me."

January 28th

A hungry bloke walks into a seedy cafe in Glasgow......
He sits at the counter and notices a Jock with his arms folded staring blankly at a bowl of chilli.

After fifteen minutes of just sitting there staring at it, the hungry bloke bravely asks, "If you aren't going to eat that, mind if I do?"

The old Jock slowly turns his head toward the young bloke and says, "Nah, ye can gae ahead."

Eagerly, the young bloke reaches over and slides the bowl over to his place and starts spooning it in with delight.

He gets nearly down to the bottom and notices a dead mouse in the chilli.

The sight was shocking and he immediately pukes up the chilli back into the bowl.

The old Jock says: - "Aye, that's as far as I got too".

January 29th

A guy goes to the supermarket and notices a very attractive woman waving at him. She says 'Hello.'

He's rather taken aback - because he can't place where he knows her from. So he asks 'Do you know me?'

To which she replies 'I think you're the father of one of my kids.'

Now his mind travels back to the only time he has ever been unfaithful to his wife. So he asks 'Are you the stripper from the bachelor party, who I made love to on the pool table, with all my buddies watching, while your partner whipped my butt with wet celery ?'

She looks into his eyes and says calmly 'No, I'm your son's teacher.'

January 30th

A nursery school pupil told his teacher he'd found a cat, but it was dead.

'How do you know that the cat was dead?' she asked her pupil.

'Because I pissed in its ear and it didn't move,' answered the child innocently.

'You did WHAT?' the teacher exclaimed in surprise.

'You know,' explained the boy, 'I leaned over and went 'Pssst' and it didn't move'

January 31st

Ralph and Edna were both patients in a mental hospital. One day while they were walking past the hospital swimming pool, Ralph suddenly jumped into the deep end. He sank to the bottom of the pool and stayed there. Edna promptly jumped in to save him. She swam to the bottom and pulled him out. When the Head Nurse Director became aware of Edna's heroic act she immediately ordered her to be discharged from the hospital, as she now considered her to be mentally stable. When she went to tell Edna the news she said, 'Edna, I have good news and bad news. The good news is you're being discharged, since you were able to rationally respond to a crisis by jumping in and saving the life of the person you love.... I have concluded that your act displays sound mindedness.

The bad news is, Ralph hung himself in the bathroom with his bathrobe belt right after you saved him. I am so sorry, but he's dead.'

Edna replied, 'He didn't hang himself, I put him there to dry..
How soon can I go home?'

'You might be an autism parent if you can quote entire Disney movies, word perfect, beginning to end because you have heard them on repeat for years.'

Rachel's spoken language is mostly echolalic. She watches and memorizes entire books and segments of videos and recites them over and over, word for word. It is frustrating really because she cannot hold a conversation with us yet she knows so many words. If she is not repeating dialogue from films her speech is mostly singular words. For example if she wants a drink she will say 'milk'. She will never ask a question and she has difficulty putting names to faces. If I am honest she probably only knows ten people by their name and the rest are known as Miss or any of the names she knows and I have lots of friends called mummy.

The really amazing thing with the Disney DVD's is that she will switch the language from English to French, Dutch, Spanish, Arabic even Chinese, bring the subtitles up in English and watch them and repeat them. She can even recite the whole of The Rescuers in French.

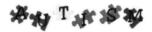

In our house there is no need to have the radio or TV on for entertaining background noise, as Rachel provides that for us. All day we hear a steady stream of repetitive dialogue from films. She also repeats lines from films/TV in public, often with hilarious timing.

She learned to jump into a swimming pool by standing on the edge of the pool, hands on hips Buzz Lightyear style and shouting, "To infinity and beyond!" which is fine if you are a 5 year old child but not so becoming in an 18 year old.

In France there is a restaurant chain called the Buffalo Grill. It is set up like a wild west saloon type place with individual booths which seat 4 or 6 people at a time. We called in there one evening for a meal and Rachel had been really quiet listening to a Toy Story tape while eating her meal up. When we got up to leave we had to pass half a dozen booths full of people eating. Kevin was way out in front as he was going to pay and Rachel was between us, with me behind her holding her shirt at the back in case she did anything unexpected. That didn't really do much, as she suddenly stopped at a booth where 6 people were sitting eating, stuck her head in the middle of them all and shouted "SHUT UP, JUST SHUT UP!" They all looked at each other and started laughing. She was being Woody!

We were shopping in a supermarket in France one day and she grabbed hold of a man, looked him straight in the face and shouted "YOU ARE A PIG!!" Lion King was the flavour of the day and she was reciting the part where Pumba turns to Timon and says "Man I'm stuffed I ate like a pig," to which Timon replies "Pumba, you *are* a pig". Fortunately for us the man didn't understand her but we giggled our way around the supermarket.

February

February 1st

Wife hit her husband over the head with a frying pan.
HUSBAND: "What was that for?"
WIFE: "I found a paper in your pocket with the name Jenny on it."
HUSBAND: "I took part in a race last week and Jenny was the name of my horse"
WIFE: "Oh, sorry!"
Next day the wife hit him with the frying pan again
HUSBAND: "What now?"
WIFE: "Your horse is on the phone"

February 2nd

A man asked an American Indian what was his wife's name.
He replied, "She is called Five Ponies".
The man said, "That's an unusual name for your wife.
Does it mean she is worth five ponies to you?"

The Old Indian answered, "No. It is old Indian Name. It mean...
NAG, NAG, NAG, NAG, NAG!"

February 3rd

An old man and woman hate each other, but remain married for years.
During their shouting fights, the old man constantly warns his wife, "If I die first, I will dig my way up and out of the grave to come back and haunt you for the rest of your life!"

One day, the man abruptly dies.
After the burial, the wife goes straight to the local bar and begins to party. Her friends ask if she isn't worried about her husband digging himself out of the grave.
The wife smiles "Let the old bugger dig. I had him buried upside down!"

February 4th
Two Irish nuns have just arrived in USA by boat, and one says to the other, "I hear that the people in this country actually eat dogs."
"Odd," her companion replies, "but if we shall live in America, we might as well do as the Americans do."
As they sit, they hear a push cart vendor yelling, "Hot Dogs, get your dogs here," and they both walk towards the hot dog cart.
"Two dogs, please!," says one. The vendor is very pleased to oblige, wraps both hot dogs in foil and hands them over.
 Excited, the nuns hurry to a bench and begin to unwrap their 'dogs.'
The mother superior is first to open hers.
She begins to blush, and then, after staring at it for a moment, leans to the other nun and in a soft brogue whispers:
"What part did you get?"

February 5th

A young ventriloquist was touring Sweden and was doing a show in a small fishing town. With his dummy on his knee, he starts going through his usual dumb blond jokes. Suddenly, a blonde woman in the fourth row stands on her chair and starts shouting, "I've heard enough of your stupid blonde jokes. What makes you think you can stereotype Swedish blonde women that way? What does the colour of a woman's hair have to do with her worth as a human being? Its men like you who keep women like me from being respected at work and in the community and from reaching our full potential as people. Its people like you that make others think that all blondes are dumb! You and your kind continue to perpetuate discrimination against not only blondes, but women in general...pathetically all in the name of humour!"

The embarrassed ventriloquist begins to apologize, and the blond yells:

"You stay out of this! I'm talking to that little pip squeak on your lap."

February 6th

I was at my bank today; there was a short line. There was just one lady in front of me, an Asian lady who was trying to exchange yen for dollars. It was obvious she was a little irritated . . .

She asked the teller, "Why it change? Yesterday, I get two hunat dolla fo yen. Today I only get hunat eighty? Why it change?"

The teller shrugged his shoulders and said, "Fluctuations"

The Asian lady says, "Fluc you white people too"

☺☺

February 7th

The nun teaching Sunday school was speaking to her class one morning and she asked the question, 'When you die and go to Heaven, which part of your body goes first?'
Suzy raised her hand and said, 'I think it's your hands.'
'Why do you think it's your hands, Suzy?'
Suzy replied: 'Because when you pray, you hold your hands together in front of you and God just takes your hands first.'
'What a wonderful answer!', the nun said.
Little Johnny raised his hand and said, 'Sister, I think it's your feet.'
The nun looked at him with the strangest look on her face.
'Now, Johnny, why do you think it would be your feet?'
Johnny said: "Well, I walked past Mom and Dad's bedroom the other night. Mom had her legs up in the air and she was saying:
'Oh, God! I'm coming!'
If Dad hadn't pinned her down, I reckon we'd have lost her."

February 8th

John O'Reilly hoisted his beer and said, "Here's to spending the rest of me life, between the legs of me wife!"
That won him the top prize at the pub for the best toast of the night!
He went home and told his wife, Mary, "I won the prize for the best toast of the night."
She said, "Aye, did ye now. And what was your toast?"

John said, "Here's to spending the rest of me life, sitting in church beside me wife."

"Oh, that is very nice indeed, John!" Mary said.

The next day, Mary ran into one of John's drinking buddies on the street corner.

The man chuckled leeringly and said, "John won the prize last night at the pub with a toast about you, Mary."

She said, "Aye, he told me, and I was a bit surprised myself. You know, he's only been in there twice in the last four years. "Once I had to pull him by the ears to make him come, and the other time he fell asleep".

February 9th

A fireman was working on the engine outside the Station, when he noticed a little girl nearby in a little red wagon with little ladders hung off the sides and a garden hose tightly coiled in the middle.

The girl was wearing a fireman's helmet.

The wagon was being pulled by her dog and her cat.

The fireman walked over to take a closer look.

'That sure is a nice fire truck,' the fireman said with admiration.

'Thanks,' the girl replied.

The fireman looked a little closer. The girl had tied the wagon to her dog's collar and to the cat's testicles.

'Little partner,' the fireman said, 'I don't want to tell you how to run your rig, but if you were to tie that rope around the cat's collar, I think you could go faster. '

The little girl replied thoughtfully, 'You're probably right, but then I wouldn't have a siren.'

☺☺

February 10th

A couple were invited to a swanky costume party. Unfortunately, the wife came down with a terrible headache and told her husband to go to the party alone. He being a devoted husband protested, but she argued and said she was going to take some aspirin and go to bed, and there was no need for his good time being spoiled by her not going.

So he took his costume and away he went.

The wife, after sleeping soundly for about an hour, awakened without pain and, since her husband did not know what her costume was, she thought she would have some fun by watching her husband to see how he acted when she was not with him.

She joined the party and soon spotted her husband cavorting around on the dance floor, dancing with every nice woman he could, and copping a little touch here and a little kiss there.

His wife sidled up to him and, being a rather seductive babe herself, he left his current partner high and dry and devoted his time to the new babe who had just arrived. She let him go as far as he wished ... naturally, since he was her husband.

Finally, he whispered a little proposition in her ear and she agreed. So off they went to one of the cars and had a quickie.

Just before unmasking at midnight, she slipped away, went home, put the costume away, and got into bed, wondering what kind of explanation he would make for his behaviour.

She was sitting up reading when he came in, and she asked what kind of a time he had. He said: "Oh, the same old thing. You know I never have a good time when you're not there."

"Did you dance much?"
"You know, I never even danced one dance.
When I got there, I met Pete, Bill, Browning, and some other guys, so we went into the den and played poker all evening.
But you're not going to believe what happened to the guy I loaned my costume to..."

☺☺

February 11th

I was in Starbuck's recently when I suddenly realized I desperately needed to fart. The music was really loud so I timed my farting with the beat of the music.
After a couple of songs I started to feel better. I finished my coffee and noticed that everyone was staring at me...
And suddenly I remembered I was listening to my iPod.

☺☺

February 12th

Hung Chow calls into work and says, "Hey, I no come work today, I sick, headache, stomach ache, legs hurt, I no come work."
The boss says, "You know something, Hung Chow, I really need you today. When I feel like this, I go to my wife and tell her to give me sex. That makes everything better and I go to work. You try that."
Two hours later Hung Chow calls again. "I do what you say, I feel great, I be in work soon...........................you got nice house."

☺☺

February 13th

Two Irish businessmen in a new shopping centre were sitting down for a break in their soon-to-be new shop...
As yet, the shop wasn't ready, with only a few shelves set up.
One said to the other, "I bet any minute now some pensioner is going to walk by, put their face to the window, and ask what we're selling."
No sooner were the words out of his mouth when, sure enough, a curious old woman walked to the window, had a peek, and in a soft voice asked, "What are you selling here?"
One of the men replied sarcastically, "We're selling arse-holes."
Without skipping a beat, the old dear said, "Must be doing well.......... Only two left!"

February 14th

I thought I'd got a late Valentines card this morning as the envelope had 'For your eyes only' on the front.
But it was just my new contact lenses.

Girl: "I can't be your valentine for medical reasons."
 Boy: "Really?"
Girl: "Yeah, you make me sick!"

February 15th

Three men were taking a trip on a plane. When they get on the pilot tells the passengers not to throw anything out of the windows. The plane lifts off and they're on their way.

On the plane the first man finds a pencil and wondering what to do with it he is told by one of the other men to throw it out the window, so he does.

Then the second guy finished his apple and wondering how to get rid of the core he asks the other two men, they tell him to throw it out the window, so he does.

Next the third man finds a grenade! Panicking he throws it out the window.

After the plane had landed the three men were walking down the street when they came across a guy holding his eye.

The three men asked him what happened, he said he had looked up in the sky and a pencil fell and hit him in the eye.

So the three men continued down the street and they come across a man holding his head, the three ask him what's wrong?

The man says that he was walking down the street and an apple core fell on his head!

Feeling a little strange the men continue down the street when they come across a man holding his stomach laughing his head off!

The three men ask him what's so funny.

The man replies, I farted and that building exploded!

February 16th

The preschool teacher says, "We're going to do vocabulary today. Who can use the word 'definitely' in a sentence?"

Mary raises her hand and exclaims, "Me, me, me!"

The teacher says, "Go ahead, what's the sentence?

Mary replies, "The sky is definitely blue."
"That's good, Mary," says the teacher, "but the sky can also be grey or white."
Sam raises his hand and states, "Grass is definitely green."
The teacher says, "That's good, Sam, but grass can be brown, too."
Little Johnny raises his hand and asks, "Do farts have lumps in them?"
The teacher says, "No Johnny, why do you ask that?"
Little Johnny replies, "Well, I've definitely pooed my pants."

February 17th

An American walks into a busy bar in Scotland and says he can drink a full bottle of whisky in under 10 seconds and challenges anyone to a race.
After a hush a wee Scotsman walks out of the pub and everyone else just carries on.................
Five minutes later the wee Scotsman walks back in and takes on the American.
They both race to drink the bottle of whisky and the wee Scotsman wins, doing it in 8 seconds.
The American says "Gee that's amazing, you're the first to beat me. But where did you go when you walked out of the pub?"
The wee Scotsman says, "I just went next door to make sure I could do it first."

February 18th

Paddy was driving down the street in a sweat because he had an important meeting to attend and he could not find a parking space.

Looking up at the sky he said, "LORD, if you find me a space I will attend mass for the rest of my life and give up my Irish whisky".

Miraculously a space appeared.

Looking up again he said," Don't bother I have found one!"

February 19th

A woman was very distraught at the fact that she had not had a date or any sex in quite some time.

She was afraid she might have something wrong with her, so she decided to employ the medical expertise of a sex therapist.

Her doctor recommended that she go see Dr Chang, the well-known Chinese sex therapist. So she went to see him.

Upon entering the examination room, Dr Chang said, "OK, take off all you crose."

The woman did as she was told.

"Now, get down and craw reery reery fass to odder side of room."

Again, the woman did as she was instructed.

Dr. Chang then said, "OK, now craw reery reery fass back to me."

So she did.

Dr Chang slowly shook his head and said, "Your probrem vewy bad - you haf Ed Zachary Disease, worse case I ever see, dat why you not haf sex or dates."

Terrified, the woman asked, "Oh my God, Dr Chang, what is Ed Zachary Disease?

Dr Chang looked the woman in the eyes and replied, "Ed Zachary disease is when your face rook Ed Zachary rike your ass."

☺☺

February 20th

An elderly couple go to a sex therapist's office. The Doctor asks, "What can I do for you?"

The man says, "Will you watch us have sexual intercourse?"

The doctor raises both eyebrows, but he is so amazed that such an elderly couple are asking for sexual advice that he agrees.

When the couple finish, the doctor says, "There's absolutely nothing wrong with the way you have intercourse".

He thanks them for coming, he wishes them good luck, he charges them £50 and he says goodbye.

The next week, however, the couple return and asks the sex therapist to watch again. The sex therapist is a bit puzzled, but agrees.

This happens several weeks in a row. The couple makes an appointment, have intercourse with no problems, pay the doctor, then leave. Finally, after 5 or 6 weeks of this routine, the doctor says, "I'm sorry, but I have to ask. Just what are you trying to find out?"

The old man says, "We're not trying to find out anything. She's married and we can't go to her house. I'm married and we can't go to my house. The Holiday Inn charges £98. The Hilton charges £139. We do it here for £50, and I get £43 back from BUPA!"

☺☺

February 21st

A blonde, a brunette, and a redhead all work at the same office for a female boss who always goes home early.

"Hey, girls," says the brunette, "let's go home early tomorrow. She'll never know."

So the next day, they all leave right after the boss does. The brunette gets some extra gardening done, the redhead goes to a bar, and the blonde goes home to find her husband having sex with the female boss! She quietly sneaks out of the house and returns at her normal time.

 "That was fun," says the brunette. "We should do it again sometime."

"No way," says the blonde. "I almost got caught."

February 22nd

A lawyer runs a stop sign and gets pulled over by a sheriff's deputy. He thinks that he is smarter than the deputy because he is a lawyer from New York and is certain that he has a better education then any cop from Houston. He decides to prove this to himself and have some fun at the deputy's expense.

Deputy says, "Licence and registration, please."

Lawyer says, "What for?"

Deputy says, "You didn't come to a complete stop at the stop sign."

Lawyer says, "I slowed down, and no one was coming."

Deputy says, "You still didn't come to a complete stop. Licence and registration, please."

Lawyer says, "What's the difference?"

Deputy says, "The difference is, you have to come to a complete stop, that's the law. Licence and registration, please!"

Lawyer says, "If you can show me the legal difference between slow down and stop, I'll give you my license and registration, and you give me the ticket. If not, you let me go and don't give me the ticket."

Deputy says, "Sounds fair. Exit your vehicle, sir."

At this point, the deputy takes out his nightstick and starts beating the crap out of the lawyer and says, "Do you want me to stop or just slow down?"

February 23rd

Mick and Paddy had promised their Uncle Seamus, who had been a seafaring gent all his life, to bury him at sea when he died.

Of course, in due time, he did pass away and the boys kept their promise.

They set off with Uncle Seamus all stitched up in a burial bag and loaded onto their rowboat.

After a while Mick says, 'Do yer tink dis is far enuff out, Paddy?'

Without a word Paddy slips over the side only to find himself standing in water up to his knees.

'Dis'll never do, Mick. Let's row some more.'

After a bit more rowing Paddy slips over the side again but the water is only up to his belly, so they row on.

Again Mick asks Paddy, 'Do yer tink dis is far enuff out Paddy?'

Once again Paddy slips over the side and almost immediately says, 'No dis'll neva do.' The water was only up to his chest.

So, on they row and row and row and finally Paddy slips over the side and disappears.

Quite a bit of time goes by and poor Mick is really getting himself into a state when suddenly Paddy breaks the surface gasping for breath.
'Well is it deep enuff yet, Paddy?'
'Aye'tis, now hand me dat shovel!'

February 24th

The boss of a big company needed to call one of his employees about an urgent problem with one of the main computers, so he dialled the employee's home phone number and was greeted with a child's whisper.
"Hello."
"Is your daddy home?" he asked.
"Yes," whispered the small voice.
"May I talk with him?"
The child whispered, "No."
Surprised, and wanting to talk with an adult, the boss asked, "Is your
Mummy there?"
"Yes."
"May I talk with her?
Again the small voice whispered, "No."
Hoping there was somebody with whom he could leave a message, the boss asked "Is anybody else there?"
"Yes," whispered the child, "a policeman."
Wondering at what a policeman would be doing at his employee's home, the boss asked, "May I speak with the policeman?"
"No, he's busy", whispered the child.
"Busy doing what?"
"Talking to Daddy and Mummy and the Fireman," came the whispered answer.

Growing concerned and even worried as he heard what sounded like a helicopter through the earpiece on the phone the boss asked, "What is that noise?"

"A hello-copper" answered the whispering voice.

"What is going on there?" asked the boss, now truly alarmed.

In an awed whispering voice the child answered, "The search team just landed the hello-copper."

Alarmed, concerned, and even more than just a little frustrated the boss asked, "What are they searching for?"

Still whispering, the young voice replied along with a muffled giggle:

"ME."

February 25th

I recently decided to try a new restaurant in town. It was quite busy and I sat at the only available table. As I sat down, I knocked the spoon off the table with my elbow. The waiter reached into his shirt pocket, pulled out a clean spoon and set it on the table.

I was impressed. "Do all the waiters carry spoons in their pockets?" I asked

He replied, "Yes sir, ever since we had that efficiency expert. He determined that 17.8% of our diners knock the spoon off the table. So by carrying clean spoons with us, we save trips to the kitchen."

I enjoyed my meal and as I was paying the waiter, I commented, "Forgive the intrusion, but do you know that you have a string hanging from your fly?"

He replied, "Yes, we all do. It seems that the same efficiency expert determined that we spend too much time washing our hands after using the men's room. So, the other end of that string is tied to my willy. When I need to go, I simply pull the string to pull out my willy, go, and return to work. Having never touched myself, there is no need to wash my hands. It saves a lot of time."

Hang on a minute," I said. "How do you get your willy back in your pants?"

The Waiter replied, "Well, I don't know about the other guys, but I use the spoon."

February 26th

Jake was dying. His wife sat at his bedside.

He looked up and said weakly: `I have something I must confess.'

`There's no need,' his wife replied.

`No', he insisted, `I want to die in peace... I slept with your sister, your best friend, her best friend and your mother!'

`Shh, I know' she replied, `Now just rest and let the poison work'.

February 27th

A married man is having an affair with his secretary.

One day they went to her place and made love all afternoon.

Exhausted, they fell asleep and woke at 8 pm.

The man hurriedly dressed and told his lover to take his shoes outside and rub them in the grass and dirt.

He put his shoes on and drove home.

`Where have you been?' demanded his wife.

`I can't lie to you,' he replied, `I'm having an affair with my secretary...we had sex all afternoon.'

She looked down at his shoes and said `You lying b******! You've been playing golf!'.

February 28th

Three Italian nuns die and go to heaven.
At the Pearly Gates, they are met by St. Peter. He says, 'Sisters, you all led such exemplary lives that the Lord is granting you six months to go back to earth and be anyone you wish to be'
The first nun says, 'I want to be Sophia Loren;' and *poof* she's gone.
The second says, 'I want to be Madonna', and *poof* she's gone.
The third says, 'I want to be Sara Pipalini..'
St. Peter looks perplexed. 'Who?', he asks.
'Sara Pipalini,' replies the nun.
St. Peter shakes his head and says, 'I'm sorry, but that name just doesn't ring a bell.'
The nun then takes a newspaper out of her habit and hands it to St. Peter. St. Peter reads the paper and starts laughing.
 He hands it back to her and says. 'No sister, the paper says it was the ' Sahara Pipeline' that was laid by 1,400 men in 6 months.'

'You might be an autism parent if you watch a movie via your child mimicking it back at you instead of watching it on TV.'

Besides reciting the dialogue Rachel also acts out the scenes and expects whoever is nearby to join in. Most people are obliging and I have had deputy head teachers lying on my floor being Pumba and Timon pretending they are full after eating too much, or dancing up and down pretending to be Barney. A doctor friend had to be a tree whilst Rachel rubbed her back up and down against her, scratching herself like Baloo the bear from the jungle book, and a few have sat quite happily while she licked their faces being Sarabi giving Simba a bath.

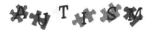

She lives and dreams children's videos and when she wakes we have to guess who she has been dreaming about. If she wakes and lies totally still with her hands clasped together on her chest and her lips pursed, she is Sleeping Beauty waiting for her kiss. If her legs spring from beneath the duvet with a wiggle and a loud shout of "Oo ooooo oh" it is Barney and Kevin has to spring through the door with a Barney voice and shout "It's Barney, oh oh oh oh!" and jump and spin around in the air. Others days she will turn to me and say "Porridge today Gromit, Tuesday" and then give a big "GERONIMO!" as she pretends to be Wallace falling through the ceiling. There have been many times when I have had to play pretend in the middle of the night. I have lost count of how many times I have been Postman Pat or Superted at 3 or 4am.

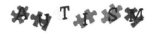

If you aren't too familiar with the way Rachel behaves then you may be in for a shock, like our friend Wilma was when she offered to look after her one day while we attended a funeral. When we went to pick her up she told us they had been sitting nicely watching 'Wallace and Gromit – A Grand Day Out' when Rachel suddenly hit her hard on the top of her head. She was copying the part where the oven hits Wallace with a truncheon, Wilma swears she saw stars. Rachel re-wound the tape to do it again but at least that time Wilma was ready for it. She also said Rachel was lying on the floor and saying she had sore legs. Wilma thought they were sore from horse riding and was massaging them to make them better. What she didn't know was Rachel was acting out the Snowman where his legs glow and start to melt after going for a ride on the motorbike. She lies down with her arms crossed under her head pretending she is in a freezer and says 'Ah, nice and warm.'

One of her favourite movies is The Land Before Time, several times we have had doctors' appointments, or gone visiting people and she has been on all fours, arms and legs straight, with her bottom in the air crawling around the floor being Littlefoot the dinosaur, whilst pretending to munch the grass, making slurping sounds and then scooting around fast shouting 'Sharp tooth!' with a worried look on her face. When she is Littlefoot I am known as 'mother' instead of the usual mummy.

March

March 1st

Be careful what you buy on eBay.

If you buy stuff on line, check out the seller carefully.

A friend has just spent £95 plus VAT on a penis enlarger.

The buggers sent him a magnifying glass.

The only instructions said, "Do not use in sunlight."

March 2nd

An Irishman was terribly overweight, so his doctor put him on a diet. 'I want you to eat regularly for 2 days, then skip a day, and repeat this procedure for 2 weeks. The next time I see you, you should have lost at least 5 pounds.'

When the Irishman returned, he shocked the doctor by having lost nearly 60lbs!

'Why, that's amazing!' the doctor said, 'Did you follow my instructions?'

The Irishman nodded....'I'll tell you though, by jaysus, I t'aut I was going to drop dead on that 3rd day.'

'From the hunger, you mean?' asked the doctor.

'No, from the bloody skippin'.

March 3rd

In a dark and hazy room, peering into a crystal ball, the fortune teller delivered grave news:

"There's no easy way to tell you this, so I'll just be blunt. Prepare yourself to be a widow. Your husband will die a violent and horrible death this year."

Visibly shaken, Laura stared at the woman's lined face, then at the single flickering candle, then down at her hands.

She took a few deep breaths to compose herself and to stop her mind racing.
She simply had to know.
She met the Fortune Teller's gaze, steadied her voice and asked, "Will I be acquitted?"

March 4th

An elderly man goes into a brothel and tells the madam he would like a young girl for the night. Surprised, she looks at the ancient man and asks how old he is.
'I'm 90 years old,' he says.
'90?' replies the woman. 'Don't you realize you've had it?'
'Oh, sorry,' says the old man. 'How much do I owe you?'

March 5th

A man walks into a bar in New York City. He orders three whiskeys. The bartender pours him one and says, "Let me know when you want the next one." But the man says, "I think you've misunderstood me. I'd like all three at once."
The bartender pours two more drinks. The man drinks down the three drinks, pays, and leaves.
This goes on almost every night for a couple of weeks.
Finally the bartender asks the man why he orders three drinks at a time, since there's no real advantage to it.
So the man tells him, "When I left the auld sod I promised my two brothers that whenever I sat down to take a taste of the creature, I'd order one for me and one for each of them. That's why I order three at once." It makes sense to the bartender, so he's satisfied.

The man keeps coming back almost every night for more than a year. He and the bartender get to know each other pretty well.

Then one day, the man orders only two drinks. This goes on for a couple weeks, but the bartender is afraid to ask if anything happened to one of the brothers.

Finally, the man comes into the bar and only orders two drinks, again. The bartender figures he has to ask, and summons up the courage to say, "I noticed you've been ordering only two drinks for the last few weeks. Is everything alight with your brothers?"

The man looks at the bartender, puzzled, and then realizes what he is implying. He smiles and says, "Yes! My brothers are fine, but I've given up drinking for Lent."

March 6th

Su Wong marries Lee Wong.

 The next year, The Wong's have a new baby. The nurse brings out a lovely, healthy, bouncy, but definitely a Caucasian, WHITE baby boy.

'Congratulations,' says the nurse to the new parents.

'Well Mr Wong, what will you and Mrs Wong name the baby?'

The puzzled father looks at his new baby boy and says, 'Well, two Wong's don't make a white, so I think we will name him..............

Sum Ting Wong!

March 7th

A salesman drove into a small town where a circus was in progress.

A sign read: 'Don't Miss Derek the Amazing Scotsman'.

The salesman bought a ticket and sat down.

There, on centre stage, was a table with three walnuts on it.

Standing next to it was an old Scotsman.

Suddenly the old man lifted his kilt, whipped out a huge willy and smashed all three walnuts with three mighty swings!

The crowd erupted in applause as the elderly Scot was carried off on the shoulders of the crowd.

Ten years later the salesman visited the same little town and saw a faded poster for the same circus and the same sign

'Don't Miss Derek the Amazing Scotsman'.

He couldn't believe the old guy was still alive, much less still doing his act!

He bought a ticket.

Again, the centre ring was illuminated.

This time, however, instead of walnuts, three coconuts were placed on the table.

The Scotsman stood before them, then suddenly lifted his kilt and shattered the coconuts with three swings of his amazing member.

The crowd went wild!

Flabbergasted, the salesman requested a meeting with him after the show.

'You're incredible!' he told the Scotsman. 'But I have to know something. You're older now, why switch from walnuts to coconuts?'

'Well laddie,' said the Scot, 'Ma eyes are no what they used t'ae be.'

☺☺

March 8th

A man breaks into a house to look for money and guns. Inside, he finds a young couple in bed. He orders the guy out of bed and ties him to a chair.

While tying the homeowner's wife to the bed, the convict gets on top of her, kisses her neck, then gets up and goes into the bathroom.

While he's in there, the husband whispers over to his wife: "Listen, this guy is an escaped convict. Look at his clothes! He's probably spent a lot of time in jail and hasn't seen a woman in years. I saw how he kissed your neck."

"If he wants sex, don't resist, don't complain. Do whatever he tells you. Satisfy him no matter how much he nauseates you. This guy is obviously very dangerous. If he gets angry, he'll kill us both. Be strong, honey. I love you!"

His wife responds:

" He wasn't kissing my neck, he was whispering in my ear.......He told me that he's gay, thinks you're cute, and asked if we had any Vaseline. I told him it was in the bathroom.

Be strong honey, I love you, too!"

March 9th

Irishman went into the confessional and said to his priest, 'I almost had an affair with another woman.'

The priest said, 'What do you mean, almost?'

The Irishman said, 'Well, we got undressed and rubbed together, but then I stopped.

The priest said, 'Rubbing together is the same as putting it in. You're not to see that woman again. For your penance, say five Hail Mary's and put £50 in the poor box.'
The Irishman left the confessional, said his prayers, and then walked over to the poor box.
He paused for a moment and then started to leave.
The priest, who was watching, quickly ran over to him saying, 'I saw that. You didn't put any money in the poor box!'
The Irishman replied, 'Yeah, but I rubbed the £50 on the box, and according to you, that's the same as putting it in!'

March 10th
A man and his wife were having some problems at home and were giving each other the silent treatment. Suddenly, the man realized that the next day, he would need his wife to wake him at 5:00 AM for an early morning business flight.
Not wanting to be the first to break the silence (and LOSE), he wrote on a piece of paper, 'Please wake me at 5:00 AM.'
He left it where he knew she would find it.
The next morning, the man woke up, only to discover it was 9:00 AM and he had missed his flight.
 Furious, he was about to go and see why his wife hadn't wakened him, when he noticed a piece of paper by the bed.
 The paper said, 'It is 5:00 AM. Wake up.'

March 11th

A married couple walks up to a wishing well. The guy leans over, makes a wish and throws in a penny.

His wife decides to make a wish, too, but she leans over too far, falls into the well and drowns.

The guy says, "Wow, it really works."

March 12th

A woman was having a passionate affair with an inspector from a pest-control company.

One afternoon they were carrying on in the bedroom together when her husband arrived home unexpectedly.

'Quick,' said the woman to the lover, 'into the closet!' and she pushed him in the closet, stark naked.

The husband, however, became suspicious and after a search of the bedroom discovered the man in the closet.

'Who are you?' he asked him.

'I'm an inspector from Bugs-B-Gone,' said the exterminator.

'What are you doing in there?' the husband asked.

'I'm investigating a complaint about an infestation of moths,' the man replied.

'And where are your clothes?' asked the husband.

The man looked down at himself and said, 'Those little buggers!'

March 13th

A 75-year-old man walked into a crowded waiting room and approached the desk. The Receptionist said, 'Yes sir, what are you seeing the Doctor for today?'

'There's something wrong with my dick', he replied.

The receptionist became irritated and said, 'You shouldn't come into a crowded waiting room and say things like that. '

'Why not, you asked me what was wrong and I told you,' he said.

The Receptionist replied; 'Now you've caused some embarrassment in this room full of people. You should have said there is something wrong with your ear or something, and discussed the problem further with the Doctor in private.'

The man replied, 'You shouldn't ask people questions in a roomful of strangers if the answer could embarrass anyone.'

The man then decided to walk out, waited several minutes, and then re-entered.

The Receptionist smiled smugly and asked, 'Yes?'

'There's something wrong with my ear,' he stated.

The Receptionist nodded approvingly and smiled, knowing he had taken her advice.

'And what is wrong with your ear, Sir?'

'I can't pee out of it,' he replied.

March 14th

A store that sells new husbands has opened in Manchester, just off Deansgate where a woman may go to choose a husband. Among the instructions at the entrance is a description of how the store operates:

You may visit this store ONLY ONCE! There are six floors and the value of the products increase as the shopper ascends the flights. The shopper may choose any item from a particular floor, or may choose to go up to the next floor, but you cannot go back down except to exit the building!

So, a woman goes to the Husband Store to find a husband. On the first floor the sign on the door reads:

Floor 1 - These men Have Jobs

She is intrigued, but continues to the second floor, where the sign reads:

Floor 2 - These men Have Jobs and Love Kids.

'That's nice,' she thinks, 'but I want more.'

So she continues upward. The third floor sign reads:

Floor 3 - These men Have Jobs, Love Kids, and are Extremely Good Looking.

'Wow,' she thinks, but feels compelled to keep going.

She goes to the fourth floor and the sign reads:

Floor 4 - These men Have Jobs, Love Kids, are Drop-dead Good Looking and Help With Housework...

'Oh, mercy me!' she exclaims, 'I can hardly stand it!'

Still, she goes to the fifth floor and the sign reads:

Floor 5 - These men Have Jobs, Love Kids, are Drop-dead Gorgeous, Help with Housework, and Have a Strong Romantic Streak.

She is so tempted to stay, but she goes to the sixth floor, where the sign reads:

Floor 6 - You are visitor 31,456,012 to this floor. There are no men on this floor. This floor exists solely as proof that women are impossible to please. Thank you for shopping at the Husband Store.

PLEASE NOTE:

To avoid gender bias charges, the store's owner opened a New Wives store just across the street with the same rules.

The first floor has wives that love sex.

The second floor has wives that love sex and have money and like beer

The third, fourth, fifth and sixth floors have never been visited.

March 15th

On the first day of school, the children brought gifts for their teacher.
The supermarket manager's daughter brought the teacher a basket of assorted fruit.
 The florist's son brought the teacher a bouquet of flowers.
The candy-store owner's daughter gave the teacher a pretty box of
candy.
 Then the liquor-store owner's son brought up a big, heavy box.
 The teacher lifted it up and noticed that it was leaking a little bit.
She touched a drop of the liquid with her finger and tasted it.
"Is it wine?" she guessed.
 "No," the boy replied.
 She tasted another drop and asked, "Champagne?"
"No," said the little boy.............."It's a puppy!"

March 16th

A guy walks into a bar with an alligator. It's about 10 feet long. The bartender flips out and says, "Hey buddy, you gotta get that son of a bitch outta here. It's going to bite one of my customers and I'm going to get sued."
The guy says, "No, no, no, it's a tame alligator. I'll prove it to you."

He picks up the alligator and puts it on the bar. Then he unzips his pants, pulls out his package and sticks it in the alligator's mouth.

The alligator just keeps his mouth open. After about 5 minutes, he pulls it out of the alligator's mouth and zips up his pants and says, "See, I told you it was a tame alligator. Anybody else want to try it?"

The drunk down at the end of the bar says, "Yeah, I'd like to try it but I don't think I can hold my mouth open that long!"

March 17th

It's Saint Patrick's Day and an armed hooded robber bursts into the Bank of Ireland and forces the tellers to load a sack full of cash. On his way out the door with the loot one brave Irish customer grabs the hood and pulls it off revealing the robber's face.

The robber shoots the man without hesitation.

He then looks around the bank to see if anyone else has seen him. One of the tellers is looking straight at him and the robber walks over and calmly shoots him dead.

Everyone by now is very scared and looking down at the floor.

"Did anyone else see my face?" screams the robber.

There is a few moments of silence then one elderly Irish gent, looking down, tentatively raises his hand and says, "I think my wife here may have caught a glimpse."

March 18th

A man goes to Spain and attends a bullfight. Afterwards he goes to a nearby restaurant and orders the specialty of the day. The waiter brings him two very big balls on a huge plate, which the tourist eats with relish.

The next day he goes to the same restaurant again, once again orders the specialty of the day, and he is brought two very big balls on a huge plate. It tastes even more scrumptious.

The third day he does the same and the fourth, but on the fifth day he goes to the restaurant and orders the specialty of the day, and they bring him two very small balls on a big plate.

 The man asks, "What gives?"

And the waiter says, "Senor, the bullfighter doesn't always win!"

March 19th

A truck driver frequently travelled through a small town where there was a courthouse at the side of the road.

Of course, there were always lawyers walking along the road so the truck driver made it a practice to hit any pedestrian lawyers with his truck as he sped by.

One day, he spotted a priest walking along the road and stopped to give him a ride.

A little further along, as he approached the town, he spotted a lawyer walking along the side of the road.

 Automatically, he veered his truck towards the lawyer, but...then he remembered his passenger.

He swerved back to the centre, but he heard a "whump" and in the rear view mirror he spotted the lawyer rolling across the field.

He turned to the priest and said, "Father, I'm sure that I missed that lawyer!"

And the priest replied, "That's OK, my son, I got him with the door.'

☺☺

March 20th

Did you hear about the cannibal who arrived late to the dinner party?

They gave him the cold shoulder!

☺☺

March 21st

The blonde walks into a drugstore and asks the pharmacist for some bottom deodorant. The pharmacist, a little bemused, explains to the woman that they don't sell anything called bottom deodorant, and never have.

Unfazed, the blonde assures him that she has been buying the stuff from this store on a regular basis, and would like some more.

"I'm sorry," says the pharmacist, "we don't have any."

"But I always get it here," says the blonde.

"Do you have the container it comes in?"

"Yes!" says the blonde, "I will go and get it."

She returns with the container and hands it to the pharmacist, who looks at it and says to her, "This is just a normal stick of underarm deodorant."

The annoyed blonde snatches the container back and reads out loud from the container: "To apply, push up bottom."

☺☺

March 22nd

A man is in bed with his wife when there is a knock at the door. He rolls over and looks at his clock, and its 3:30 in the morning.

"I'm not getting out of bed at this time," he thinks, and rolls over.

Then a louder knock follows. "Aren't you going to answer that?" says his wife.

So he drags himself out of bed and goes downstairs. He opens the door and there is a man standing on the porch. It didn't take the homeowner long to realize the man was drunk.

"Hi there," slurs the stranger. "Can you give me a push??"

"No, get lost! It's half past three. I was in bed," says the man and he slams the door.

He goes back up to bed and tells his wife what happened and she says, "That wasn't very nice of you. Remember that night we broke down in the pouring rain on the way to pick the kids up from the babysitter and you had to knock on that man's house to get us started again? What would have happened if he'd told us to get lost?"

"But the guy was drunk," says the husband.

"It doesn't matter," says the wife. "He needs our help and it would be the Christian thing to help him."

So the husband gets out of bed again, gets dressed, and goes downstairs. He opens the front door, and not being able to see the stranger anywhere he shouts, "Hey, do you still want a push?"

He hears a voice cry out, "Yeah, please."

So, still being unable to see the stranger he shouts, "Where are you?"

And the drunk replies, "Over here, on the swing."

☺☺

March 23rd
Two men both drag their right foot as they walk.
As they meet, one man looks at the other knowingly, points to his foot and says, "Iraq 2003."
The other points his thumb behind him and says, "Dog muck, 20 feet back."

☺☺

March 24th
A young woman dressed in shorts had been taking golf lessons. She had just started playing her first round of golf when she suffered a bee sting. Her pain was so intense that she decided to return to the clubhouse for help ... and to complain.
Her golf pro saw her come into the clubhouse and asked, "Why are you back in so early? What's wrong?"
"I was stung by a bee," she said.
"Where," he asked.
"Between the first and second hole," she replied.
He nodded knowingly and said, "Then your stance is too wide."

☺☺

March 25th
An old lady goes to the doctor and says, "I have this problem with frequent gas. Fortunately, the farts never smell and are always silent. As a matter of fact, I've farted at least 10 times since I've been here, and I bet you didn't even notice!"
The doctor says, "I see. Take these pills and come back next week."
The next week the old lady returns.

"Doctor," she says, "I don't know what the hell you gave me, but now my silent farts stink like the dickens."
The doctor says, "Good! Now that we've cleared up your sinuses, let's work on your hearing."

March 26th

How did Captain Hook die?
He wiped his bum with the wrong hand!!

March 27th

An army major visiting the sick soldiers goes up to one private and asks:
"What's your problem, Soldier?"
"Chronic syphilis, Sir"
"What treatment are you getting?"
"Five minutes with the wire brush each day."
"What's your ambition?"
"To get back to the front, Sir."
"Good man." says the Major.
He goes to the next bed. "What's your problem, Soldier?"
"Chronic piles, Sir"
"What treatment are you getting?"
"Five minutes with the wire brush each day."
"What's your ambition?"
"To get back to the front, Sir."
"Good man." says the Major.
He goes to the next bed. "What's your problem, Soldier?"
"Chronic gum disease, Sir"
"What treatment are you getting?"
"Five minutes with the wire brush each day."

"What's your ambition?"
"To get the wire brush before the other two, Sir"

March 28th
During a recent password audit at our company, it was found that a blonde receptionist was using the following password:
MickeyMinniePlutoHueyLouieDeweyDonaldGoofyParis
When asked why she had such a long password, she said she was told that it had to be at least 8 characters long and include at least one capital.

March 29th
There was a brave with no sexual experience. He went to the chief and asked to meet one of his daughters. The chief said, "No, you first must go into the forest and practice on the trees."
The little brave did as he was told.
After several days, the brave returned and asked again, "Chief, can I meet with one of your daughters?"
"Why sure you can, young brave," said the chief.
So, after a little foreplay with the chief's daughter, the little brave undressed her.
Before going any further, he turned around, grabbed a stick, and started pushing it in and out of her.
"What do you think you're doing?" she screamed.
"Checking for bees," he replied.

March 30th

Little Johnny asks his mother her age.
She replies, "Gentlemen don't ask ladies that question."
Johnny then asks his mother how much she weighs.
Again his mother replies, "Gentlemen don't ask ladies that question."
The boy then asks, "Why did Daddy leave you?"
To this, the mother says, "You shouldn't ask that," and sends him to his room.
On the way, Johnny trips over his mother's purse.
When he picks it up, her driver's licence falls out.
Johnny runs back into the room. "I know all about you now. You are 36 years old, weigh 127 pounds and Daddy left you because you got an 'F' in sex!"

March 31st

One day Mum was cleaning her son's room and in the wardrobe she found a bondage S&M magazine.
This was highly upsetting for her.
She hid the magazine until his Father got home and showed it to him.
He looked at it and handed it back to her without a word.
So she asked him, "What should we do about this?"
Dad looked at her and said, "Well I don't think you should spank him."

'You might be an autism parent if your child watches advertisements on repeat and can recite them word for word

We don't watch a lot of television in our house so most of the advertisements Rachel has memorised are what she has seen on old videotapes that she watches on repeat. As you will see I have heard them that many times I also know them word for word.

In Rachel's last year at school when she was 19 years old they asked me to write down five things that I would like Rachel to learn to do that year. I wrote - learn to zip her coat up and fasten buttons, to sharpen a pencil by herself and to learn her address and phone number. The first two she can now do, albeit with difficulty, sharpening a pencil is just too complicated and the last two will never happen because of two advertisements, namely Disneyland Paris and an advertisement on one of her Rosie and Jim videos.

Despite repeating our phone number to her over and over and even making a song up with the numbers in it, if you were to say to Rachel 'What is your phone number?' her response would be '0990030303, someone you know can't wait to go. Disneyland Paris the land where wishes come true.'

Always the whole advertisement, never just the number.

Ask her for her address and she will say 'Rosie and Jim ragdolls are available from – Rosie and Jim Department, Oxfam Trading, Murdoch Road, Bicester, Oxon, OX6 7RF, price £19.95 each plus postage and packing.'

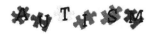

The warning at the beginning of DVD's is also a favourite of hers that will get played and rewound over and over. She will put a pair of glasses on and say 'Whenever you rent or buy a video you need to be sure the film that you choose is suitable for the audience at home. To help you there are certificates given to films to tell you broadly what the film is like. This film has been classified U (she understands this U to mean 'you' and will point at herself). This means quite simply, universal, in other words it can be seen by all people of all ages, there will be nothing unsuitable for children and the whole family might enjoy it. Video certificates are there to give you a chance to make an informed choice, they allow you to have peace of mind and be entertained. Thanks for listening, enjoy the film.'

Every time we go past the cleaning section in the supermarket she will ask for a bottle of fabric softener which she calls baby because of the picture on the bottle. She gets really excited and flaps her hands and when she has it in her hand she will say 'Everybody feels good in Lenor' and grin. This is the one product that HAS to be bought every time we shop and I know I will never run out of.

If she sees the Fairy washing powder she says 'Next to skin it's not just fairly soft but Fairy soft.'

If she spots a CIF bottle we have to stop and look until she has recited another advertisement which ends with a shout of 'That's the power of CIF!'

Shopping in ASDA is a nightmare thanks to their pocket patting advertisements. Despite our best attempts to stop her she always seems to smack people's bottoms when we are preoccupied. She doesn't care who they are either, old, young, fat, thin if she can get a smack in she will and it is usually when someone is bending over to pick something up off the bottom shelf. The look on some people's faces is priceless, and some of them have probably never moved as fast in all their lives, but they are all usually understanding after an apology. One day we were in a shoe shop and the assistant bent down to pick a pair of shoes up off the shelf. Rachel patted her bottom and the assistant turned in a hurry and glared at us. Kevin and I both pointed at Craig, who went crimson with embarrassment and protested his innocence. It was naughty of us I know, but very funny when the assistant joined in by shaking her head at him whilst tut- tutting and shaking a finger at him.

April

April 1st

A father passing by his son's bedroom, was astonished to see the bed was nicely made, and everything was picked up. Then, he saw an envelope propped up prominently on the pillow. It was addressed, 'Dad.'

With the worst premonition, he opened the envelope and read the letter, with trembling hands.

'Dear, Dad. It is with great regret and sorrow that I'm writing to you. I had to elope with my new girlfriend, because I wanted to avoid a scene with Mum and you. I've been finding real passion with Stacy, and she is so nice, but I knew you would not approve of her, because of all her piercing's, tattoos, her tight Motorcycle clothes, and because she is so much older than I am.

But it's not only the passion, Dad. She's pregnant. Stacy said that we will be very happy. She owns a trailer in the woods, and has a stack of firewood for the whole winter. We share a dream of having many more children.

Stacy has opened my eyes to the fact that marijuana doesn't, really hurt anyone. We'll be growing it for ourselves, and trading it with the other people in the commune, for all the cocaine and ecstasy we want.

In the meantime, we'll pray that science will find a cure for AIDS, so Stacy can get better. She sure deserves it!

Don't worry Dad, I'm 15, and I know how to take care of myself. Someday, I'm sure we'll be back to visit, so you can get to know your many grandchildren.

Love, your son, Joshua.

P.S . Dad, none of the above is true. I'm over at Jason's house. I just wanted to remind you that there are worse things in life than the school report that's on the kitchen table.

Call when it is safe for me to come home.

☺☺

Autism awareness day!

Q. What goes red, red, red, red, red, red, red.
Yellow, yellow, yellow, yellow, yellow, yellow.
Blue, blue, blue, blue, blue, blue.
Green, green, green, green, green?

A. An autistic persons lego house.

☺☺

Q. What's the autistic theme song?
A. If you're happy and you know it, flap your hands.

☺☺

April 3rd

Little Johnny's first grade class was playing "Name That Animal." The teacher held up a picture of a cat and asked, "What animal is this?"
"A cat!" said Suzy.
"Good job. Now, what's this animal?"
"A dog!" said Ricky.
"Good. Now what animal is this?" she asked, holding up a picture of a deer.
The class fell silent. After a couple of minutes, the teacher said, "It's what your mom calls your dad."
"I know!" called out Little Johnny. "A horny bugger!"

☺☺

April 4th

Shortly after having her ninth baby, an Irish Catholic woman runs into her parish priest.

He congratulates her on the new offspring and says, "Nine children is certainly a full house."

"Well," she replies, "I don't know how I get pregnant so often. It must be something in the air."

"Yes," says the priest, "your legs."

April 5th

Two blondes were driving down the road.

The blonde driving looks at her friend in the passenger seat and asks her to see if her indicator is working.

So the blonde looks out the window and says, "Yes. No. Yes. No."

April 6th

One day, a farmer was tending to his livestock when he noticed that one of his cows was completely cross-eyed. He called up a veterinarian friend of his who told him to bring in his cow.

The vet took one look at the cow, stuck a tube up the cow's butt, and blew into the tube until the cow's eyes straightened out.

The vet charged the farmer a hundred bucks, and the farmer went home happy.

About a week later, the cow's eyes were cross-eyed again, but this time the farmer figured he could probably take care of it himself. So he called his hired hand over, and together they put a tube up the cow's butt.

The farmer put his lips to the tube and started to blow. Strangely, nothing happened, so he asked his hired hand to give it a try.

The hired hand removed the tube, turned it around, put it in the cow's butt and started to blow.

"What are you doing?" asked the farmer, horrified.

"Well, I wasn't gonna use the side that YOU had put your lips on."

April 7th

A woman tells her friend she is getting married for the fourth time.

"How wonderful! I hope you don't mind me asking, what happened to your first husband?"

"He ate poisonous mushrooms and died."

"Oh, how tragic! What about your second husband?"

"He also ate poisonous mushrooms and died."

"Oh, how terrible! I'm almost afraid to ask you about your third husband."

"He died of a broken neck."

"A broken neck?"

"He wouldn't eat the mushrooms."

April 8th

It's the first day of kindergarten, and the teacher decides to do taste association.

"I'll blindfold you and give you a sweet, and you tell me what flavour it is," she tells the children.

So she gives them all a cherry flavour, and says, "What flavour is that?"

The whole class answers, "Mmmm, that's cherry."
"Very good," the teacher replies.
So she gives them all an orange and they reply, "Mmm, that's orange."
"Very good," she says again.
Then she gives them all a honey flavour.
The whole class sits perplexed by the strange taste, so the teacher says, "OK, I'll give you a hint, it's something your parents might call each other."
Billy spits his out on the floor and yells, "Spit 'em out everyone, they're ASSHOLES!"

April 9th
A Welshman, an Englishman and an Irishman were being chased by Farmer Giles with a shotgun. After 10 minutes of running they spotted a barn and ran inside.
Once inside they each hid in an old sack against the barn wall. The farmer went into the barn but did not see where they went.
He was about to turn back when he saw three suspicious looking sacks. He walked forward and prodded the first sack with his gun. The Englishman inside said... "Meow'.'
"Just cats," he thought.
He then prodded the second sack. The Welshman, hearing how the Englishman got off said... "Woof'.'
"Just dogs," he thought.
As he walked towards the last sack, the Irishman worked out what he was going to say.
As soon as the farmer prodded his sack he said...
"Potatoes!"

April 10th

A man was packing for his business trip and his three year old daughter was having a wonderful time playing on the bed.

At one point she said, 'Daddy, look at this', and stuck out two of her fingers.

Trying to keep her entertained, he reached out and stuck her tiny fingers in my mouth and said,

'Daddy's gonna eat your fingers,' and pretended to eat them.

He went back to packing, looked up again and his daughter was standing on the bed staring at her fingers with a devastated look on her face.

He said, 'What's wrong, honey?'

She replied, 'What happened to my bogey?'

April 11th

One afternoon the pastor came to call on the church organist and she showed him into her quaint sitting room. She invited him to have a seat while she prepared tea.

As he sat facing her old Hammond organ, the young minister noticed a cut-glass bowl sitting on top of it. The bowl was filled with water, and in the water floated, of all things.................A CONDOM!!!

When she returned with tea and scones, they began to chat.

The pastor tried to stifle his curiosity about the bowl of water and its strange floater, but soon it got the better of him and he could no longer resist.

"Miss Beatrice", he said, "I wonder if you would tell me about this?" pointing to the bowl.

"Oh, yes," she replied, "Isn't it wonderful? I was walking through the Park a few months ago and I found this little package on the ground. The directions said to place it on the organ, keep it wet and that it would prevent the spread of disease. Do you know I haven't had the flu all winter!"

April 12th

An old farmer went to town to see a movie. The ticket agent asked, "Sir, what's that on your shoulder?"
The old farmer said, "That's my pet rooster Chucky, wherever I go, Chucky goes."
"I'm sorry sir." said the ticket agent, "We don't allow animals in the theatre."
The old farmer went around the corner and stuffed the bird down his pants. He returned to the booth, bought a ticket and entered the theatre. He sat down next to two old widows named Mildred and Marge.
The movie started and the rooster began to squirm. The old farmer unzipped his pants so Chucky could stick his head out and watch the movie.
"Marge", whispered Mildred.
"What", said Marge.
"I think this guy next to me is a pervert.", said Mildred.
"What makes you think that", asked Marge.
"He unzipped his pants and he has his thing out", whispered Mildred.
"Well, don't worry about it", said Marge, "At our age we've seen them all."
"I thought so", said Mildred, "But this one is eating my popcorn!"

☺☺

April 13th

After living in the remote countryside of Ireland all his life, an old Irishman decided it was time to visit Dublin.

In one of the stores, he picks up a mirror and looks into it. Not ever having seen a mirror before, he remarked at the image staring back at him.

'How about that! He exclaims, 'Here's a picture of me Fadder.'

He bought the mirror thinking it was a picture of his dad, but on the way home he remembered his wife didn't like his father, so he hung it in the shed, and every morning before leaving to go fishing, he would go there and look at it.

His wife began to get suspicious of his many trips to the shed.

So, one day after her husband left, she went to the shed and found the mirror.

As she looked into the glass, she fumed, 'So that's the ugly bitch he's running around with.'

April 14th

One day Harry the eagle waited at the nest for Mary, his darling of 10 glorious years.

When she didn't return he went looking for her and found her.

She had been shot. Dead!

Harry was devastated, but after about six minutes of mourning he decided that he must get himself another mate but since there weren't any lady eagles available he'd have to cross the feather barrier.

So he flew off to find a new mate.

He found a lovely dove and brought her back to the nest.

The sex was good, but all the dove would say is "I am a little DOVE, I want a little love! I am a little DOVE, I want a little love!"

Well this got on Harry's nerves so he kicked the dove out of the nest and flew off once more to find a mate.

He soon found a very sexy loon and brought her back to the nest. Again the sex was good but all the loon would say is, "I am a LOON, I want to spoon! I am a LOON, I want to spoon!"

So out went the loon.

Once more he flew off to find a mate.

This time he found a gorgeous duck and he brought the duck back to the nest. This time the sex was great, but all the duck would say was.....

(scroll down)

v

v

v

v

v

v

v

v

v

v

No, the duck didn't say THAT

... Don't be SO disgusting. !

The duck said, "I am a little DRAKE, you made a BIG MISTAKE!!!!!!!!!!

☺☺

April 15th

A farmer was in a bar drinking and looking all depressed. His friend asked him why he was looking depressed and he replied, "Some things you just can't explain. This morning I was outside milking. As soon as the bucket was full the cow kicked it down with her left foot so I tied her left leg to a pole.

I began to fill up the bucket again and she kicked it down with her right foot, so I tied her right leg to a pole too.

As soon as I finished milking her again she knocked down the bucket with her tail and I took off my belt and tied up her tail with my belt.

As I was tying up her tail, my pants dropped down, and then my wife came out and well, trust me, some things you just can't explain!"

April 16th

A couple drove down a country road for several miles, not saying a word.

An earlier discussion had led to an argument and neither of them wanted to concede their position.

As they passed a barnyard of mules, goats, and pigs,

The husband asked sarcastically, 'Relatives of yours?'

'Yep,' the wife replied, 'in-laws.'

April 17th

Q: How can you tell a blonde's been using the computer?

A: There's Tippex all over the screen.

☺☺

April 18th

An old couple celebrates their 50th wedding anniversary in their home.

The old man says, "Just think 50 years ago we were sitting here at this same breakfast table, naked as new-borns."

"Well," the old lady snickers, "what do you say -- should we get naked?"

The two immediately strip to the buff and sit back down at the table.

"You know, honey," the little old lady says slyly, "My breasts burn for you now as they did 50 years ago."

"I'm not surprised," replies the old man. "One's in your coffee and the other is in your porridge!"

April19th

A very tired nurse walks into a bank, totally exhausted after an 18-hour shift.

Preparing to write a cheque, she pulls a rectal thermometer out of her purse and tries to write with it. When she realizes her mistake, she looks at the flabbergasted teller, and without missing a beat, she says:

"Well, that's great....that's just great..........some asshole's got my pen!"

☺☺

April 20th

Once upon a time there was a man who was peacefully driving down a winding road. Suddenly, a bunny skipped across the road and the man couldn't stop.

He hit the bunny head on.

The man quickly jumped out of his car to check the scene. There, lying lifeless in the middle of the road, was the Easter Bunny.

The man cried out, "Oh no! I have committed a terrible crime! I have run over the Easter Bunny!"

The man started sobbing quite hard and then he heard another car approaching.

It was a woman in a red convertible.

The woman stopped and asked what the problem was.

The man explained, "I have done something horribly sad. I have run over the Easter Bunny. Now there will be no one to deliver eggs on Easter Sunday, and it's all my fault."

The woman ran back to her car.

A moment later, she came back carrying a spray bottle. She ran over to the motionless bunny and sprayed it.

The bunny immediately sprang up, ran into the woods, stopped, and waved back at the man and woman.

Then it ran another 10 feet, stopped, and waved. It then ran another 10 feet, stopped, and waved again. It did this over and over and over again until the man and the woman could no longer see the bunny.

Once out of sight, the man exclaimed, "What is that stuff in that bottle?"

The woman replied, "It's harespray. It revitalizes hare and adds a permanent wave."

☺☺

April 21st

A husband and wife go to a restaurant. The waiter approaches the table to take their order.

"I'll have your biggest, juiciest steak," says the husband.

"But sir, what about the mad cow?" asks the waiter.

"Oh," says the husband, "she'll order for herself."

April 22nd

A girl invites her boyfriend over for dinner with her parents. Since this is such a big event, the girl tells him that after dinner she wants to have sex with him for the first time. The boy is ecstatic, but nervous because he's a virgin.

He goes to the chemist to get some condoms. He tells the pharmacist his situation and asks for advice. The pharmacist tells him everything there is to know about sex.

At the register, the pharmacist asks how many condoms he'd like to buy: a 3-pack or a 10-pack. The boy says he feels lucky and insists on the 10-pack.

That night, the boy shows up for dinner a little late.

His girlfriend meets him at the door leads him straight to the dinner table where her parents are already seated.

The boy sits down, quickly offers to say grace and bows his head.

A minute passes, and the boy is still silent with his head down. Five minutes pass, and still no movement from the boy.

Finally, after 10 minutes, the girlfriend leans over and whispers to the boy, "I had no idea you were this religious."

The boy turns and whispers back, "I had no idea your father was a pharmacist."

April 23rd

A housewife buys a parrot to keep her company during the day.

The clerk warns that the parrot was donated by a brothel, where he may have picked up some colourful language.

The housewife doesn't mind and brings the parrot home.

When she uncovers the cage, the parrot says, "Brawkk! New Madam. Hello Madam."

When her three daughters come home from school, the parrot says, "Brawkk! New Girls. Hello Girls."

Finally, her husband, Phil, comes home from work, just in time for dinner.

When he walks past the parrot, the parrot says, "Brawkk! Hi Phil!"

April 24th

An old man goes to his doctor and says, "I don't think my wife's hearing is as good as it used to be. What should I do?"

The doctor replies, "Try this test to find out for sure. When your wife is in the kitchen doing dishes, stand 15 feet behind her and ask her a question. If she doesn't respond keep moving closer, asking the question until she hears you."

The man goes home and sees his wife preparing dinner.

He stands 15 feet behind her and says, "What's for dinner, honey?"

No response.

He moves to 10 feet behind her and asks again -- no response.

Five feet, no answer.

Finally, he stands directly behind her and asks, "Honey, what's for supper?"

She says, "For the fourth time, I SAID CHICKEN!"

April 25th

Mummy, what were you doing bouncing on Daddy's stomach last night?"

"I have to do that, or Daddy's belly gets very fat. Bouncing keeps him skinny."

"That's not going to work."

"Why not?"

"Because the babysitter keeps blowing him back up again."

April 26th

William and Mildred decided to celebrate their 40th wedding anniversary with a trip to Las Vegas. William went to the front desk to check them in while Mildred stayed with the car. As he was leaving the lobby, a young woman dressed in a very short skirt introduced herself as Candie. William brushed her off.

When William and Mildred got to their room, he told her that he'd been approached by a prostitute.

"I don't believe you," laughed Mildred.

"I'll prove it," said William. He called down to the desk and asked for Candie to come to room 1217.

"Now," he said, "you hide in the bathroom with the door open just enough to hear us."

Soon, there was a knock on the door. Candie walked in, swirling her hips provocatively. "So, I see you're interested after all," she said.

William asked, "How much do you charge?"

"$125 basic rate, $100 tips for special services."

William was taken aback. "$125! I was thinking more in the range of $25."

Candie laughed. "You must really be an old-timer if you think you can buy sex for that price."

"Well," said William, "I guess we can't do business. Goodbye."

After she left, Mildred came out of the bathroom. "I just can't believe it."

William said, "Let's go have a drink and forget it."

Back downstairs at the bar, the old couple sipped their cocktails.

Candie came up behind William, pointed at Mildred, and said, "See what you get for $25?"

April 27th

A beautiful princess comes upon a frog in a meadow near her castle.

The frog hops into the princess' lap and says, "My lady, one kiss from you, and I will turn back into the dapper, young prince that I once was, and then, my sweet, we can marry and set-up housekeeping in yon castle with my mother, where you can prepare my meals, clean my clothes, bear my children and forever be happy doing so."

That night, as the princess dines on lightly sautéed frog legs, she chuckles to herself, "I don't bloody think so."

April 28th

An old woman buys herself some bright red crotchless panties and goes home to surprise her husband.

When her husband comes home, she calls him into the bedroom and points to her new panties. "Hey old timer", she says, "Come and get some of this!"

The old man says, "Hell no, woman. It done ate a hole in your drawers!"

April 29th

'I went to the zoo the other day; there was only one dog in it.

It was a shitzu.'

April 30th

A man would come home very late and very drunk every night. His wife decides to teach him a lesson by dressing up like Satan and scaring him.

When he finally stumbles across the lawn, his wife jumps out and howls like a demon.

He looks at her and slurs, "You don't scare me. I'm married to your sister!"

☺☺

'You might be an autism parent if you get excited when your child swears because at least they said something!'

Rachel adores Beatrix Potter stories. She is very even tempered and rarely gets annoyed, but she knows that Mrs Macgregor gets annoyed with her husband John in the Flopsy Bunny episode. To let Rachel know she is upsetting us we tell her she is making us sad and sign an upside down mouth. She understands that you say sorry when you have done something wrong but I don't think she really understands what sorry means. She will often sign sorry and say sorry mummy/daddy and then turn around and whisper "John MacGregor" in an angry voice. She will also say it out of frustration too. We think it is her version of swearing!

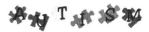

Rachel loves looking on YouTube at videos. She will hold a video in her hand and copy the letters of the title one by one and type them into the computer to look for the videos she wants to watch. Postman Pat is one of her favourites. Unfortunately some people dub over the original script with swearing. In one episode, A Windy Day, Pat is driving along and a tree has blown down blocking the road. In the dubbed version Pat slams on his brakes and shouts "Oh look out, oh shit!" We were driving along one day approaching traffic lights when a car in front switched lanes. Kevin had to brake suddenly and Rachel shouted "OH SHIT!" Needless to say Kevin braked hard quite a few times to get her to say it again. It is now her party trick, we say "What does Postman Pat say?" and she shouts "Oh Shit!" and everyone laughs. One night we were at a quiz night, and Jo who runs the quiz has known Rachel for many years, she shouted, "This question is for Rachel – What is the name of Postman Pats cat?" Rachel shouted "Oh Shit!" and everyone in the place fell about laughing.

Fortunately for us that is the limit of her cursing, besides 'John MacGregor of course. ;)

May

May 1st

A college math professor and his wife are both 60 years old.

One evening the wife comes home and finds a note from her husband.

It says: "My dear, now that you are 60 years old, there are some things you no longer do for me. I am at the Holiday Inn with my 20-year-old student. Don't bother waiting up for me."

He returns home late that night to find a note from his wife:

"You, my dear, are also 60 years old and there are also things I need that you're not giving me. So, I am at the Ramada with one of your 20-year-old students. Being a maths professor, I'm sure you know that 20 goes into 60 more times than 60 goes into 20.

So, don't YOU wait up for ME."

May 2nd

After an intense high speed chase, a police officer finally gets the lawbreaker to pull over.

"You know," says the cop, "I was originally pulling you over to tell you your tail light is out. Why the hell did you take off like that?"

"Last week my wife ran off with a cop," the man said, "and I was afraid you were trying to give her back."

May 3rd

The local news station was interviewing an 80-year-old lady because she had just gotten married for the fourth time.

The interviewer asked her questions about her life, about what it felt like to be marrying again at 80, and then about her new husband's occupation.

"He's a funeral director," she answered.

"Interesting," the newsman thought... He then asked her if she wouldn't mind telling him a little about her first three husbands and what they did for a living.

She paused for a few moments, needing time to reflect on all those years.

After a short time, a smile came to her face and she answered proudly, explaining that she had first married a banker when she was in her 20's, then a circus ringmaster when in her 40's, and a preacher when in her 60's, and now - in her 80's - a funeral director.

The interviewer looked at her, quite astonished, and asked why she had married four men with such diverse careers.

(Wait for it)

She smiled and explained, "I married one for the money, two for the show, three to get ready, and four to go."

May 4th

Dave's wife thinks that he is pushing himself too hard, so she takes him to a local strip club for his birthday.

The doorman at the club greets them and says, "Hey, Dave! How are ya?"

His wife is puzzled and asks if he's been to this club before.

"Oh no," says Dave. "He's on my bowling team."

They sit and a waitress asks Dave if he'd like his usual.

His wife is becoming uncomfortable and says, "You must come here a lot for that woman to know what you drink."

"No, honey, she's in the Ladies Bowling League. We share lanes with them."

A stripper comes over to their table and throws her arms around Dave. "Hi, Davey," she says, "Want your usual lap dance?"

Dave's wife, now furious, grabs her purse and storms out of the club. Dave follows and spots her getting into a cab. Before she can slam the door, he jumps in beside her.

His wife starts screaming at him.

The cabbie turns his head and says, "Looks like you picked up a real doozy this time, Dave!"

May 5th

A man said to his wife one day, 'I don't know how you can be so stupid and so beautiful all at the same time.'

'The wife responded, 'Allow me to explain. God made me beautiful so you would be attracted to me; God made me stupid so I would be attracted to you!'

May 6th

The CIA has three candidates, two men and a woman, for one assassin position.

On the final day of testing, the CIA proctor leads the first male candidate to a large steel door and hands him a gun.

"We must know that you will follow our instructions, regardless of the circumstances," he explains. "Inside this room, you will find your wife sitting in a chair. Take this gun and kill her."

The man is horrified, "You can't be serious! I could never shoot my wife!"

"Well," says the proctor, "you're definitely not the right man for this job then."

The CIA proctor leads the second male candidate to another large steel door and hands him a gun.

"We must know that you will follow instructions, no matter what the circumstances," the proctor explains. "Inside this room, you will find your wife sitting in a chair. Take this gun and kill her."

The second man steadies himself, takes the gun and enters the room. After three quiet minutes, the man exits the room with tears in his eyes. "I wanted to do it -- I just couldn't pull the trigger and shoot my wife. I guess I'm not the right man for the job."

Finally, the CIA proctor leads the female candidate to yet another large steel door and hands her a gun.

"We must be sure that you will follow instructions, no matter what the circumstances. Inside this room, you will find your husband sitting in a chair. Take this gun and kill him."

The woman takes the gun, enters the room, and before the door even closes completely behind her, she's fired off six shots. Then all hell breaks loose behind the door -- cursing, screaming, and crashing. Suddenly, all goes quiet. The door opens slowly, the woman exits, and wiping the sweat from her brow, she says, "Did you guys know the gun was loaded with blanks? I had to beat him to death with the chair!"

May 7th

A guy buys his first motorcycle. The dealer tells him to keep a jar of Vaseline handy to rub on the chrome before it rains to prevent rusting.

A few months later, the young man's girlfriend invites him to dinner at her parents' house. Before they go in, she explains their family tradition that whoever speaks first after dinner must do the dishes.

After dinner, everyone sits in silence waiting for the first person to break. After 15 minutes, the young man decides to speed things up. He leans over and kisses his woman in front of her family. No one says a word.

Emboldened, he throws her on the table and has sex with her.

Silence.

Desperate, he grabs her mother and has sex with her on the table.

Suddenly, they hear thunder rumble in the distance. The guy thinks of his bike and, instinctively, pulls the jar of Vaseline out of his pocket.

"OK, OK," says the father, "I'll do the dishes!"

☺☺

May 8th

A man asks his mute friend what he wants in a woman.
The mute friend points to his head.
 His friend says, "Yes, intelligence is important."
Then, the mute friend rubs his thumb on the palm of his hand.
 His friend nods and says, "Certainly a woman with money would be nice."

Then, the mute friend opens his hands wide in front of him, cups his fingers and makes a bouncing motion.
His friend looks at him strangely.
"What the heck do you want a woman with arthritis for?"

May 9th
Bloke from Barnsley with piles asks chemist, "Nah then lad, does tha sell arse cream?"
Chemist replies, "Aye, Magnum or Cornetto."

May 10th
Two couples are playing cards. John accidentally drops some cards on the floor. When he bends down under the table to pick them up, he notices that Bill's wife isn't wearing any underwear.
Later, John goes into the kitchen to get some refreshments. Bill's wife follows him and asks, "Did you see anything that you liked under there?"
John admits that he did. She says, "You can have it, but it will cost you $100."
They decide that John should come to her house around 2 p.m. on Friday while Bill is at work.
On Friday, John arrives at 2 p.m. He pays Bill's wife $100. They go to the bedroom, have sex and then John leaves.
When Bill comes home at 6 p.m., he asks his wife, "Did John come by this afternoon?"
Reluctantly, she replies, "Yes, he did stop by for a few minutes."
Next Bill asks, "Did he give you $100?"

She thinks, "Oh hell, he knows!" Finally she says, "Well, yes, he did give me $100."
"Good," Bill says. "John came by the office this morning and borrowed $100 from me. He said that he would stop by our house on his way home and pay me back."

May 11th

Paddy finds a sandwich with two wires sticking out of it. He phones the police and says "Bejesas I've just found a sandwich that looks like a bomb."
The operator asks, "Is it tickin?
Paddy says "No I tink it's beef"

May 12th

An atheist was taking a walk through the woods, admiring all that evolution had created.
"What majestic trees! What powerful rivers! What beautiful animals!" he said to himself.
As he was walking along the river, he heard a rustling in the bushes behind him. When he turned to see what the cause was, he saw a 7-foot grizzly charging right towards him.
He ran as fast as he could. He looked over his shoulder and saw that the bear was closing.
He ran even faster, crying in fear. He looked over his shoulder again, and the bear was even closer.
His heart was pounding and he tried to run even faster. He tripped and fell on the ground.

He rolled over to pick himself up, but saw the bear right on top of him, reaching for him with his left paw and raising his right paw to strike him.

At that moment, the Atheist cried out "Oh my God!...."
Time stopped. The bear froze. The forest was silent. Even the river stopped moving.

As a bright light shone upon the man and a voice came out of the sky - "You deny my existence for all of these years; teach others I don't exist; and even credit creation to a cosmic accident. Do you expect me to help you out of this predicament? Am I to count you as a believer?"

The atheist looked directly into the light and said, "It would be hypocritical of me to suddenly ask you to treat me as Christian now, but perhaps could you make the bear a Christian?"

"Very well," said the voice.

The light went out. The river ran again. And the sounds of the forest resumed.

And then the bear dropped his right paw, brought both paws together, bowed his head and spoke:

"Lord, for this food which I am about to receive, I am truly thankful."

May 13th

One day, leaning on the bar, Jack says to Mike "My elbow hurts like hell. I suppose I'd better see a Doctor!"

Listen, don't waste your time down at the surgery," Mike replies

'There's a new diagnostic computer at Tesco Pharmacy. Just give it a urine sample and the computer will tell you what's wrong, and what to do about it. It takes ten seconds and only costs five quid.....a lot quicker and better than a doctor and you get Club card points".

So Jack collects a urine sample in a small jar and takes it to Tesco.

He deposits five pounds and the computer lights up and asks for the urine sample. He pours the sample into the slot and waits. Ten seconds later, the computer ejects a printout: "You have tennis elbow. Soak your arm in warm water and avoid heavy activity. It will improve in two weeks".

That evening while thinking how amazing this new technology was, Jack began wondering if the computer could be fooled. He mixed some tap water, a stool sample from his dog, urine samples from his wife and daughter and the cat, and masturbated into the mixture for good measure.

Jack hurried back to Tesco, eager to check what would happen. He deposited five pounds, poured in his concoction, and awaited the results.

The computer whirred for a little longer than he expected then printed the following:

1) Your tap water is too hard. Get a water softener.

2) Your cat's having kittens. Get a vet

3) Your dog has ringworm. Bathe him with anti-fungal shampoo.

4) Your daughter has a cocaine habit. Get her into rehab.

5) Your wife is pregnant with twins; they aren't yours. Get a lawyer.

6) And if you don't stop playing with yourself, your elbow will never get better...

Thank you for shopping at Tesco.

☺☺

May 14th

At 85 years of age, Wally married Anne, a lovely 25 year old. Since her new husband is so old, Anne decides that after their wedding she and Wally should have separate bedrooms, because she is concerned that her new but aged husband may over exert himself if they spend the entire night together.

After the wedding festivities Anne prepares herself for bed and the expected 'knock' on the door. Sure enough the knock comes, the door opens and there is Wally, her 85 year old groom, ready for action...

They unite as one. All goes well, Wally takes leave of his bride, and she prepares to go to sleep.

After a few minutes, Anne hears another knock on her bedroom door, and it's Wally. Again he is ready for more 'action.' Somewhat surprised, Anne consents for more frantic coupling. When the newlyweds are done, Wally kisses his bride, bids her a fond goodnight and leaves.

She is set to go to sleep again, but, aha, you guessed it..... Wally is back again, rapping on the door, and is as fresh as a 25-year-old, ready for more 'action.'

And, once again they enjoy each other in the way only two people in the first flush of lust can... But as Wally gets set to leave again, his young bride says to him, 'I am thoroughly impressed that at your age you can perform so well and so often. I have been with guys less than a third of your age who were only good once. You are truly a great lover, Wally.'

Wally, somewhat embarrassed, turns to Anne and says: 'You mean I've been here already?'

☺☺

May 15th

A father and his son go into the grocery store when they happen upon the condom aisle. The son asks his father why there are so many different boxes of condoms.

The father replies, "Well, you see that 3-pack? That's for when you're in high school. You have 2 for Friday night and 1 for Saturday night."

The son then asks his father, "What's the 6-pack for?"

The father replies, "Well, that's for when you're in college. You have 2 for Friday night, 2 for Saturday night, and 2 for Sunday morning."

Then the son asks his father what the 12-pack is for.

The father replies, "Well, that's for when you're married. You have one for January, one for February, one for March, one for....."

May 16th

When Dan found out he was going to inherit a fortune when his sickly father died, he decided he needed a woman to enjoy it with.

So one evening he went to a singles bar where he spotted the most beautiful woman he had ever seen. Her natural beauty took his breath away.

"I may look like just an ordinary man," he said as he walked up to her, "but in just a week or two, my father will die, and I'll inherit 20 million dollars."

Impressed, the woman went home with him that evening and, three days later, she became his stepmother.

May 17th

A sweet little girl is out in the back garden, digging a big deep hole.

A neighbour looks over the fence and says: "Why are you digging that big deep hole?"

"My goldfish died," the sweet little girl says, with a sob.

"I'm really sorry to hear that," the neighbour says, "but why such a big deep hole for a goldfish?"

The little girl gives him an evil look. "Because it's inside your bloody cat."

May 18th

"What on earth is that counting?" asked my friend Anthony as we passed the high security mental health unit in rural London

I could just about hear it...

"17...17 ...17...17...17..."

Tony was too curious to resist, he rushed at the fence and tried to jump and see over it but it was much too high so he found a small hole in the wooden panels and looked through it...

He jumped back clutching his face in agony, "Some idiots poked me in the eye with a sharp stick!"

"18...18...18...18...18..." came the sound from inside the walls...

May 19th

A young blonde Portsmouth girl, down on her luck, decided to end it all one night by casting herself into the cold, dark waters off Gunwharf Quay.

As she stood on the edge, pondering the infinite, a young sailor noticed her as he strolled by. 'You're not thinking of jumping, are you babes?' he asked.

'Yes, I am.' replied the sobbing girl.

Putting his arm around her, the kind sailor coaxed her back from the edge. 'Look, nothing's worth that. I'll tell you what; I'm sailing off for Australia tomorrow. Why don't you stow away on board and start a new life over there. I'll set you up in one of the lifeboats on the deck, bring you food and water every night and I'll look after you if you look after me- if you know what I mean. You just have to keep very quiet so that you won't be found'.

The girl, having no better prospects, agreed, and the sailor sneaked her on board that very night.

For the next 3 weeks the sailor came to her lifeboat every night, bringing food and water, and making love to her until dawn.

Then, during the fourth week, the captain was performing a routine inspection of the ship and its lifeboats. He peeled back the cover to find the startled blonde, and demanded an explanation

The girl came clean, 'I've stowed away to get to Australia . One of the sailors is helping me out. He set me up in here and brings me food and water every night and he's screwing me.'

The captain stared at her for a moment before he replied, 'He certainly is love. This is the Isle of Wight Ferry'

May 20th

One day Charlie goes into a chemist shop, reaches into his pocket and takes out a small Irish whiskey bottle and a teaspoon.

He pours some whiskey onto the teaspoon and offers it to the chemist.

"Could you taste this for me, please?"

The chemist takes the teaspoon, puts it in his mouth, swills the liquid around and swallows it.

"Does that taste sweet to you?" says Charlie.

"No, not at all," says the chemist.

"Oh that's a relief," says Charlie.

"The doctor told me to come here and get my urine tested for sugar."

May 21st

An attractive blonde from Cork, Ireland, arrived at the casino. She seemed a little intoxicated and bet twenty thousand dollars in a single roll of the dice.

She said, "I hope you don't mind, but I feel much luckier when I'm completely nude."

With that, she stripped from the neck down, rolled the dice and with an Irish brogue yelled, "Come on, baby, Mama needs new clothes!"

As the dice came to a stop, she jumped up and down and squealed. "Yes! Yes! I won, I won!"

She hugged each of the dealers, picked up her winnings and her clothes and quickly departed.

The dealers stared at each other dumbfounded.

Finally, one of them asked, "What did she roll?"

The other answered, "I don't know-I thought you were watching."

MORAL OF THE STORY

Not all Irish are drunks, not all blondes are dumb,

.....but all men....are men!

☺☺

May 22nd

In 1990 there were two Mexicans who had been lost in the desert for weeks, and they're at death's door. As they stumble on, hoping for salvation in the form of an oasis or something similar, they suddenly spy, through the heat haze, a tree off in the distance.

As they get closer they can see that the tree is draped with rasher upon rasher of bacon. There's smoked bacon, crispy bacon, life-giving juicy nearly-raw bacon, all sorts.

"Hey, Pepe" says the first bloke, "Ees a bacon tree!!! We're saved!!!"

"You're right, amigo!" says Pepe.

So Pepe goes on ahead and runs up to the tree salivating at the prospect of food. But as he gets to within five feet of the tree, there's a huge volley of gun fire, and he is shot down in a hail of bullets.

His friend quickly drops down on the sand and calls across to the dying Pepe.

"Pepe!! Pepe!! Que pasa hombre?"

With his dying breath Pepe calls out...."Ugh...run, amigo, run!!

...Ees not a Bacon Tree!"

...

...

"Ees... a.... Ham bush"

☺☺

May 23rd

A blonde cop stops a blonde motorist and asks for her driving license.

The Motorist scuffles around in her purse and can't find it. She says to the cop, "I must have left it at home officer." The cop says, "Well, do you have any kind of identification?"

The motorist scuffles around in her purse, and finds a pocket mirror. She looks at it and says to the cop, "All I have is this picture of me."

The cop says, "Ok Let me see it, then."

So the blonde motorist gives the mirror to the blonde cop, she looks at it, and replies, "Well, if I had known you were a police officer, I wouldn't have even pulled you over. You can go now."

May 24th

A woman decides to have a facelift for her birthday. She spends $5,000 and feels pretty good about the results. On her way home she stops at a newsstand to buy a paper. Before leaving, she asks the sales clerk, "I hope you don't mind my asking, but how old do you think I am?"

"About 32", the clerk replies.

"I'm actually 47," the woman says happily.

A little while later, she goes into McDonald's, and upon getting her order, asks the counter girl the same question. She replies, "I'd guess about 29."

The woman replies, "Nope, I am 47." Now she is feeling really good about herself.

While waiting for the bus home, she asks an old man the same question. He replies, "I'm 78 and my eyesight is starting to go. Although, when I was young, there was a sure way to tell how old a woman was, but it requires you to let me put my hands up your shirt and feel your boobs. Then I can tell exactly how old you are."

They waited in silence on the empty street until curiosity got the best of the woman, and she finally said, "What the hell, go ahead."

The old man slips both hands up her shirt, under her bra, and begins to feel around. After a couple of minutes, she says, "Okay, okay, how old am I?"

He removes his hands and says, "You are 47."

Stunned, the woman says, "That is amazing! How did you know?"

The old man replies, "I was behind you in line at McDonald's."

May 25th

A guy was in a cave, looking for treasure. He found an old lamp, rubbed it, and a genie came out.

The genie said "I will grant you three wishes, but your ex-wife will get double."

The man agreed, and said "I wish I had a mansion." The genie granted it, and his ex-wife got two mansions.

The man said "I would like a million dollars." The genie again granted it and his ex-wife got two million dollars.

Then the man said, "Scare me half to death."

May 26th

A man and a woman were sitting beside each other in the first class section of an airplane. The woman sneezed, took out a tissue, wiped her nose, and then visibly shuddered for ten to fifteen seconds.

The man went back to his reading. A few minutes later, the woman sneezed again, took a tissue, wiped her nose, and then shuddered violently once more.

Assuming that the woman might have a cold, the man was still curious about the shuddering. A few more minutes passed when the woman sneezed yet again.

As before she took a tissue, wiped her nose, her body shaking even more than before.

Unable to restrain his curiosity, the man turned to the woman and said, 'I couldn't help but notice that you've sneezed three times, wiped your nose and then shuddered violently. Are you OK?'

'I am sorry if I disturbed you, I have a very rare medical condition; whenever I sneeze I have an orgasm. '

The man, more than a bit embarrassed, was still curious. I have never heard of that condition before' he said. 'Are you taking anything for it?'

The woman nodded, 'Pepper.'

May 27th

Joey and Katie are sitting in school. Katie is sleeping and the teacher asks her a question. "Katie, who created Heaven and Earth?"

Joey sees Katie sleeping and quickly pokes her with a sharp pencil.

"Jesus Christ almighty!!" exclaimed Katie.

"Correct." says the teacher.

So the next day the same incident occurs and the same question comes up "Who created Heaven and Earth?"

Katie (sleeping again) is poked by Joey's pencil.

"Jesus Christ almighty!" she exclaims.

"Correct again." says the teacher.

So the next day, for a 3rd time, the teacher asks Katie "What did Eve say to Adam when she had so many children?"

Katie (sleeping again) is poked by Joey's pencil again, and screams "If you stick that thing in me one more time I am going to break it in half".

May 28th

Tony, a Para, was stationed overseas, when he received a 'Dear John' letter from his girlfriend, back in Blighty.

It read as follows:-

My Dear Tony,

I can no longer continue our relationship. The distance between us is just too great.

I must admit that I have cheated on you twice since you've gone and it is not fair to either of us to carry on like this.

I'm very sorry, but could you please return the picture that I gave you when we parted and you went away?

Love Suzie.

The Para, with obviously hurt feelings, asked his fellow Para's for any snapshots that they could spare of their girlfriends, sisters, ex-girlfriends, aunts, cousins, etc.

In addition to the picture of Suzie, Tony included the other pictures of the pretty girls that he had collected from his buddies.

There were 57 photos in the envelope......along with this note.

Dear Suzie,

I am sorry, but I cannot quite remember who you are.

Please take your picture from the pile enclosed and return the rest to me.

Take care, Tony.

☺☺

May 29th

A lady goes to her parish priest one day and tells him, "Father, I have a problem. I have two female parrots but they only know how to say one thing."

"What do they say?" the priest inquired.

"They say, 'Hi, we're prostitutes. Do you want to have some fun?" "That's obscene!" the priest exclaimed, "I can see why you are embarrassed." He thought for a minute and then said, "You know, I may have a solution to this problem. I have two male parrots who I have taught to pray and read the Bible.

Bring your two parrots over to my house and we will put them in the cage with Francis and Job. My parrots can teach your parrots to praise and worship. I'm sure your parrots will stop saying that phrase in no time."

"Thank you," the woman responded, "this may very well be the solution."

The next day, she brought her female parrots to the priest's house. As he ushered her in, she saw this two male parrots were inside their cage, hold their rosary beads and praying.

Impressed, she walked over and placed her parrots in with them.

After just a couple of seconds, the female parrots exclaimed out in unison, "Hi, we're prostitutes. Do you want to have some fun?"

There was a stunned silence. Finally, one male parrot looked over at the other male parrot and said, "Put the beads away, Francis, our prayers have been answered!"

☺☺

May 30th

Little Johnnie's neighbour had a baby. Unfortunately, the baby was born without ears.

When mother and new baby came home from the hospital, Johnnie's family was invited over to see the baby.

Before they left their house, little Johnnie's dad had a talk with him and explained that the baby had no ears.

His dad also told him that if he so much mentioned anything about the baby's missing ears or even said the word ears, he would get the smacking of his life when they came back home.

Little Johnnie told his dad he understood completely.

When Johnnie looked in the crib he said, "What a beautiful baby."

The mother said, "Why, thank you, Little Johnnie.

Johnnie said, "He has beautiful little feet and beautiful little hands, a cute little nose and really beautiful eyes. Can he see?"

"Yes", the mother replied, "we are so thankful; the Doctor said he will have 20/20 vision."

"That's great", said little Johnnie, "coz he'd be buggered if he needed glasses".

May 31st

An elderly married couple scheduled their annual medical examination the same day so they could travel together.

After the examination, the doctor then said to the man: "You appear to be in good health. Do you have any medical concerns that you would like to discuss with me?"

"In fact, I do," said the man. "After I have sex with my wife the first time, I am usually hot and sweaty. And then, after

I have sex with my wife the second time, I am usually cold and chilly."

"This is very interesting," replied the doctor. "Let me do some research and get back to you."

After examining the elderly lady, the doctor said:

"Everything appears to be fine. Do you have any medical concerns that you would like to discuss with me?"

The lady replied that she had no questions or concerns.

 The doctor than asked: "Your husband had an unusual concern. He claims that he is usually hot and sweaty after having sex the first time with you and cold and chilly after the second time."

 "Do you know why?"

"Oh that old buzzard!" she replied. "That's because the first time is usually in July and the second time is usually in December."

"You might be an autism parent if you have the same song playing every day for months on end and Christmas music isn't just seasonal but all year round.'

I can certainly relate to this one!

I think Rachel first took a liking to the group The Beautiful South because of the artwork on the cover of the album Blue is the Colour. She took a real shine to it and we had it in cassette and CD version. When we visited people's houses she would rifle through their CD collections to see if they had a copy and would invariably come home with their copy because she didn't understand that it belonged to them and wasn't hers. The first song on the album is titled Don't Marry Her. There are two versions to this song, one is the radio version and the other is the album version. The radio version lyrics are – Don't marry her love me, whereas the album version is – Don't marry her f**k me. The latter version is the version that Rachel took a liking to and played every day, over and over at a high volume so wherever we went people heard it. She also learnt to sing it, and it took a lot of loud intervention singing from us to get her to sing "love me".

My mother nearly died from embarrassment the day she had a barbecue for a few friends and family at her house. Kevin had borrowed an amp so that we could have a karaoke. Unbeknown to us Rachel's Beautiful South was in amongst the CD's and she had a mini meltdown until we put it on. Of course it had to be played as loud as possible a few times over and it certainly gave the members of the bowling club next to my mum's house something to talk about when she next went in! We breathed a collective sigh of relief the day she "found" Lionel Ritchie although The Beautiful South still pops up from time to time.

Rachel also plays Christmas songs all year round. I can remember driving to the South of France on holiday one summer and being stuck in a traffic jam in the Var where it was 40C and having Frosty the Snowman on repeat play. Unfortunately it didn't help to cool the car down at all.

June

June 1st

A minister decided that a visual demonstration would add emphasis to his Sunday sermon.

Four worms were placed into four separate jars.

The first worm was put into a container of alcohol.

The second worm was put into a container of cigarette smoke.

The third worm was put into a container of chocolate syrup.

The fourth worm was put into a container of good clean soil.

At the conclusion of the sermon, the Minister reported the following results:

The first worm in alcohol - Dead.

The second worm in cigarette smoke - Dead

Third worm in chocolate syrup - Dead

Fourth worm, in good clean soil - Alive.

So the Minister asked the congregation – "What can you learn from this demonstration?"

Maxine was setting in the back, quickly raised her hand and said, 'As long as you drink, smoke and eat chocolate, you won't have worms!'

June 2nd

A retired gentleman went into the social security office to apply for Social Security. After waiting in line a long time he got to the counter. The woman behind the counter asked him for his drivers' license to verify his age. He looked in his pockets and realized he had left his wallet at home.

He told the woman that he was very sorry but he seemed to have left his wallet at home. "Will I have to go home and come back now?" he asks.

The woman says, "Unbutton your shirt."

He opens his shirt revealing lots of curly silver hair.

She says, "That silver hair on your chest is proof enough for me.", and she processes his Social Security application.

When he gets home, the man excitedly tells his wife about his experience at the Social Security office.

She says, "You should have dropped your pants, you might have qualified for disability, too."

June 3rd

A woman went to her doctor. The doctor, after an examination, sighed and said, "I've some bad news. You have cancer, and you'd best put your affairs in order."

The woman was shocked, but managed to compose herself and walk into the waiting room where her daughter had been waiting.

"Well daughter, we women celebrate when things are good, and we celebrate when things don't go so well. In this case, things aren't well I have cancer. Let's head to the club and have a martini."

After 3 or 4 martinis, the two were feeling a little less sombre.

There were some laughs and more martinis.

They were eventually approached by some of the woman's old friends, who were curious as to what the women were celebrating.

The woman told her friends they were drinking to her impending end. "I've been diagnosed with AIDS."

The friends were aghast and gave the woman their condolences.

After the friends left, the woman's daughter leaned over and whispered, "Momma, I thought you said you were dying of cancer, and you just told your friends you were dying of AIDS."

The woman said, "I don't want any of them sleeping with your father after I'm gone."

June 4th

This blonde goes to the Western Union office and says, "I just have to get an urgent message to my mother in Europe."

The clerk says it will be $100, and she replies "But I don't have any money.... and I must get a message to her, it's urgent!... I'll do anything to get a message to her."

The clerk replies "Anything?"

"Yes.... ANYTHING!" replies the blonde.

He leads her back to his office and closes the door. He tells her to kneel in front of him.

"Unzip me..." She does.

"Take it out..... Go ahead." She does this as well.

She looks up at him, his willie in her hands and he says "Well... go ahead... do it..."

She brings her lips close to it and shouts "Hello... Mum?"

June 5th

There were two nuns...

One of them was known as Sister Mathematical (SM),

And the other one was known as Sister Logical (SL).

It is getting dark and they are still far away from the convent.

SM: Have you noticed that a man has been following us for the past thirty-eight and a half minutes? I wonder what he wants.

SL: It's logical He wants to rape us.

SM: Oh, no! At this rate he will reach us in 15 minutes at the most! What can we do?

SL: The only logical thing to do of course is to walk faster.

SM: It's not working.

SL: Of course it's not working. The man did the only logical thing. He started to walk faster, too.

SM: So, what shall we do? At this rate he will reach us in one minute.

SL: The only logical thing we can do is split. You go that way and I'll go this way. He cannot follow us both.

So the man decided to follow Sister Logical.

Sister Mathematical arrives at the convent and is worried about what has happened to Sister Logical.

Then Sister Logical arrives.

SM: Sister Logical! Thank God you are here! Tell me what happened!

SL: The only logical thing happened. The man couldn't follow us both, so he followed me

SM: Yes, yes! But what happened then?

SL: The only logical thing happened. I started to run as fast as I could and he started to run as fast as he could.

SM: And?

SL: The only logical thing happened. He reached me

SM: Oh, dear! What did you do?

SL: The only logical thing to do. I lifted my dress up.

SM: Oh, Sister! What did the man do?

SL: The only logical thing to do. He pulled down his pants.

SM: Oh, no! What happened then?

SL: Isn't it logical, Sister?
A nun with her dress up can run faster than a man with his pants down.

June 6th

Wife: 'What are you doing?'
Husband: "Nothing."
Wife: 'Nothing . . . ? You've been studying our marriage certificate for quite some time.'
Husband: 'I was looking for the expiration date.'

June 7th

A 5-year old boy went to visit his grandmother one day. While playing with his toys in her bedroom while grandma was dusting furniture, he looked up and said, "Grandma, how come you don't have a boyfriend?"
Grandma replied, "Honey, my TV is my boyfriend. I can sit in my bedroom and watch it all day long. The TV evangelists keep me company and make me feel so good. The comedies make me laugh. I'm so happy with my TV as my boyfriend."
 Grandma turned on the TV and the picture was horrible. She started adjusting the knobs trying to get the picture in focus. Frustrated, she started hitting on the backside of the TV hoping to fix the problem.
 The little boy heard the doorbell ring so he hurried to open the door.
When he opened the door, there stood Grandma's minister.

The minister said, "Hello son is your grandma home?"
The little boy replied, "Yeah, she's in the bedroom banging her boyfriend."

☺☺

June 8th
A BLONDE and a brunette are walking past a flower shop.
The brunette sees her boyfriend inside and says: "Oh no, my boyfriend is inside buying me flowers again."
The blonde asks: "Why is that so bad?"
The brunette says: "Every time he buys me flowers, he expects something in return and I don't feel like spending the entire weekend with my legs in the air."
The blonde asks: "Why, don't you have a vase?"

☺☺

June 9th
A man is lying in bed in a hospital with an oxygen mask over his mouth. A young auxiliary nurse appears to sponge his face and hands.
"Nurse," he mumbles from behind the mask, "Are my testicles black?"
Embarrassed the young nurse replies, "I don't know, I'm only here to wash your face and hands."
He struggles again to ask, "Nurse, Are my testicles black?"
Again the nurse replies, "I can't tell. I'm only here to wash your face and hands."
The ward sister was passing and saw the man getting a little distraught so she marched over to inquire what was wrong.
"Sister," he mumbled, "Are my testicles black?"

Being a nurse of longstanding, the sister was undaunted. She whipped back the bedclothes, pulled down his pyjama trousers, had a good look, pulled up the pyjamas, replaced the bedclothes and announced, "Nothing is wrong with them!!!"

At this the man pulled off his oxygen mask and asked again, "Are my test results back???

June 10th

A small zoo in Alabama acquires a rare gorilla, who quickly becomes agitated. The zookeeper determines that the female ape is in heat, but there are no male apes available for mating.

The zookeeper approaches a redneck janitor with a proposition. "Would you be willing to have sex with this gorilla for $500?" he asks.

The janitor accepts the offer, but only on three conditions: "First, I don't want to have to kiss her. And second, you can never tell anyone about this."

The zookeeper agrees to the conditions and asks about the third.

"Well," says the janitor, "I'm gonna need another week to come up with the $500."

June 11th

Little Johnny greeted his mother at the door after she had been out of town all week.

Johnny said, "Mommy, guess what? Yesterday, I was playing in the closet in your bedroom and Daddy came into the room with the lady from next door and they got undressed and they got into bed and then Daddy got on top of her and --"

The mother held up her hand and said, "Not another word! Wait until your father gets home, and then I want you to tell him exactly what you've just told me."

The father came home, and the wife told him that she was leaving him.

"But why?" croaked the husband.

"Go ahead, Johnny. Tell Daddy just what you told me."

"Well," said little Johnny, "I was playing in your closet and Daddy came upstairs with the lady next door and they got undressed and they got into bed and Daddy got on top of her and they did just what you did, Mommy, with Uncle Bob when Daddy was away last summer!"

June 12th

An old man sitting at the mall watched a teenager intently. The teenager had spiked hair in all different colours: green, red, orange, and blue. The old man kept staring at him.

When the teenager was tired of being stared at, he sarcastically asked, "What's the matter, old man? Never did anything wild in your life?"

The old man did not bat an eye when he responded, "Got drunk once and had sex with a peacock. I was just wondering if you were my son."

<u>June 13th</u>

A man died in a horrible fire. The mortician thought it was George, but the body was so badly burned that somebody would need to make a positive identification. That task fell to George's two friends, Joe and Al.

Joe: "He's burnt pretty bad, all right. Roll him over."

Joe looked at the dead man's buttocks and said, "Nope, that ain't George."

Thinking the incident strange, the mortician straightened up the body and said nothing. He brought in Al.

Al: "Wow, he's burnt to a crisp. Roll him over."

Again, "Nope, that ain't George."

Mortician: "How can you tell?"

Al: "George had two assholes."

Mortician: "What? How could he have two assholes?"

Al: "Everybody knew George had two assholes. Whenever the three of us would go into town you'd hear people say, "Here comes George with those two assholes!"

<u>June 14th</u>

A couple was golfing one day on a very, very exclusive golf course, lined with million dollar houses. On the third tee the husband said, "Honey, be very careful when you drive the ball don't knock out any windows. It'll cost us a fortune to fix."

The wife teed up and shanked it right through the window of the biggest house on the course. The husband cringed and said, "I told you to watch out for the houses. Alright, let's go up there, apologize and see how much this is going to cost."

They walked up, knocked on the door, and heard a voice say, "Come on in." They opened the door and saw glass all over the floor and a broken bottle lying on its side in the foyer. A man on the couch said, "Are you the people that broke my window?"

"Uh, yeah. Sorry about that," the husband replied.

"No, actually I want to thank you. I'm a genie that was trapped for a thousand years in that bottle. You've released me. I'm allowed to grant three wishes -- I'll give you each one wish, and I'll keep the last one for myself."

"OK, great!" the husband said. "I want a million dollars a year for the rest of my life." "No problem-it's the least I could do. And you, what do you want?" the genie said, looking at the wife. "I want a house in every country of the world," she said.

"Consider it done," the genie replied.

"You know what, genie, maybe we can repay you by making one of YOUR wishes come true... what's your wish, genie?" the husband said.

"Well, since I've been trapped in that bottle, I haven't had sex with a woman in a thousand years. My wish is to sleep with your wife."

The husband looks at the wife and said, "Well, we did get a lot of money and all those houses, honey. I guess I don't care."

The genie took the wife upstairs and ravished her for two hours.

After it was over, the genie rolled over, looked at the wife, and said, "How old is your husband, anyway?"

"35," she replied.

"And he still believes in genies? That's amazing!"

☺☺

June 15th

A psychiatrist was conducting a group therapy session with four young mothers and their small children. "You all have obsessions," he observed.

To the first mother, he said, "You are obsessed with eating. You've even named your daughter Candy."

He turned to the second Mom. "Your obsession is money. Again, it manifests itself in your child's name, Penny,"

He turned to the third Mom. "Your obsession is alcohol. Again, it manifests itself in your child's name, Brandy."

At this point, the fourth mother got up, took her little boy by the hand and whispered, "Come on, Dick, let's go".

June 16th

The big game hunter walked in the bar and bragged to everyone about his hunting skills. The man was undoubtedly a good shot and no one could dispute that. But then he said that they could blindfold him and he would recognize any animal's skin from its feel, and if he could locate the bullet hole he would even tell them what calibre the bullet was that killed the animal. The hunter said that he was willing to prove it if they would put up the drinks, and so the bet was on. They blindfolded him carefully and took him to his first animal skin. After feeling it for a few moments, he announced "Bear." Then he felt the bullet hole and declared, "Shot with a .308 rifle." He was right.

They brought him another skin, one that someone had in their car trunk. He took a bit longer this time and then said, "Elk, Shot with a 7mm Mag rifle. He was right again. Through the night, he proved his skills again and again, every time against a round of drinks. Finally he staggered home, drunk out of his mind, and went to sleep. The next morning he got up and saw in the mirror that he had one hell of a shiner. He said to his wife, "I know I was drunk last night, but not drunk enough to get in a fight and not remember it. Where did I get this black eye?"

His wife angrily replied, "I gave it to you. You got into bed and put your hand down my panties. Then you fiddled around a bit and loudly announced, "Skunk, killed with an axe."

June 17th

Muldoon lived alone in the Irish countryside with only a pet dog for company. One day the dog died, and Muldoon went to the parish priest and asked, 'Father, my dog is dead. Could ya' be saying' a mass for the poor creature?'

Father Patrick replied, 'I'm afraid not; we cannot have services for an animal in the church. But there are some Baptists down the lane, and there's no tellin' what they believe. Maybe they'll do something for the creature.'

Muldoon said, 'I'll go right away Father. Do ya' think £5,000 is enough to donate to them for the service?'

Father Patrick exclaimed, 'Sweet Mary, Mother of Jesus! Why didn't ya tell me the dog was Catholic?'

June 18th

Superman's had a hard week of fighting crime in Metropolis and is ready for some R&R. So Friday afternoon he looks up his pals Batman and Spiderman to see if they're up for going on the prowl that evening. Both turn him down on account of prior commitments and

Superman is pretty ticked. As he's flying around the stratosphere letting off steam, he spots Wonder Woman lying on her back stark naked sunbathing on the beach. "Hey," he thinks, "I'm Superman and I don't need those two clowns to have a good time. I can just fly down there at the speed of light, catch a quickie and fly away before she knows what happened."
So, Superman zips down, takes advantage of the situation and flies away at the speed of light.
Wonder Woman says, "What the hell was that?"
The Invisible Man says, "I don't know but it hurt like hell"

June 19th
An old man and an old woman met at a retirement home. They had been dating for quite some time now and one day the old man asks, "If I pull out my willie, would you hold it?"
 The woman agrees and so every day they would sit on a bench in the garden and the woman would hold the man's willie.
One day the woman went to the garden early and found the man with another woman.
She approached the man and asked what the other woman has that she doesn't.
The man replied gleefully "Parkinson's"!

June 20th
A man is driving down a deserted stretch of highway when he notices a sign out of the corner of his eye. It reads:
SISTERS OF ST. FRANCIS

HOUSE OF PROSTITUTION
10 MILES

He thinks it was just a figment of his imagination and drives on without a second thought. Soon he sees another sign which says:

SISTERS OF ST. FRANCIS
HOUSE OF PROSTITUTION
5 MILES

Suddenly, he begins to realize that these signs are for real. Then he drives past a third sign saying:

SISTERS OF ST, FRANCIS
HOUSE OF PROSTITUTION
NEXT RIGHT

His curiosity gets the best of him and he pulls into the drive. On the far side of the parking lot is a sombre stone building with a small sign next to the door reading:

SISTERS OF ST. FRANCIS

He climbs the steps and rings the bell. The door is answered by a nun in a long black habit, who asks, "What may we do for you, my son?"

He answers, "I saw your signs along the highway, and was interested in possibly doing business."

"Very well my son. Please follow me."

He is led through many winding passages and is soon quite disoriented. The nun stops at a closed door, and tells the man,

"Please knock on this door."

He does as he is told and this door is answered by another nun in long habit, holding a tin cup. This nun instructs, "Please place $50 in the cup, and then go through the large wooden door at the end of this hallway."

He gets $50 out of his wallet and places it in the second nun's cup. He trots eagerly down the hall and slips through the door, pulling it shut behind him. As the door locks

behind him, he finds himself back in the parking lot, facing another small sign:
GO IN PEACE
YOU HAVE JUST BEEN SCREWED
BY THE SISTERS OF ST. FRANCIS

June 21st

A man takes his wife to the stock show. They start heading down the alley that had the bulls. They come up to the first bull and his sign stated: "This bull mated 50 times last year." The wife turns to her husband and says, "He mated 50 times in a year, you could learn from him."
They proceed to the next bull and his sign stated: "This bull mated 65 times last year." The wife turns to her husband and says, "This one mated 65 times last year. That is over 5 times a month. You can learn from this one, also."
They proceeded to the last bull and his sign said: "This bull mated 365 times last year." The wife's mouth drops open and says, "WOW! He mated 365 times last year. That is ONCE A DAY!!! You could really learn from this one."
The man turns to his wife and says, "Go up and inquire if it was 365 times with the same cow."

June 22nd

A guy out on the golf course takes a high speed ball right in the crotch. Writhing in agony, he falls to the ground, when he finally gets himself to the doctor.
He says, "How bad is it doc? I'm going on my honeymoon next week and my fiancée is still a virgin in every way."

The doc said , "I'll have to put your penis in a splint to let it heal and keep it straight. It should be okay next week."

So he took four tongue depressors and formed a neat little 4-sided bandage, and wired it all together; an impressive work of art.

The guy mentions none of this to his girl, marries, and on his honeymoon night in the motel room, she rips open her blouse to reveal a gorgeous set of breasts. This was the first time he saw them.

She says, "You are my FIRST, no one has ever touched these breasts."

He whips down his pants and says... "Look at this; it's still in the CRATE!"

June 23rd

Grandma and Grandpa were watching a healing service on the television. The evangelist called to all who wanted to be healed to go to their television set, place one hand on the TV and the other hand on the body part where they wanted to be healed.

Grandma got up and slowly hobbled to the television set, placed her right hand on the set and her left hand on her arthritic shoulder that was causing her to have great pain.

Then Grandpa got up, went to the TV, and placed his right hand on the set and his left hand on his crotch.

Grandma scowled at him and said, "I guess you just don't get it. The purpose of doing this is to heal the sick, not to raise the dead!"

☺☺

June 24th

The City Health Inspector walks into a new restaurant unannounced and takes a seat where he can see the kitchen.

While he is sitting there, an order goes back for a pizza. The chef appears and the Health Inspector nearly chokes when he see that he is not wearing a shirt. The chef then proceeded to grab a lump of pizza dough and press it out flat on his bare chest.

Appalled, the Health Inspector had barely finished writing up this infraction when an order came back for a hamburger. The cook proceeded to grab a handful of ground meat and pressed it into a perfect patty in his armpit.

Shocked and bewildered, the Health Inspector called for the manager and explained the gravity of the deplorable conditions he had seen.

"That's nothing," said the manager, "you should come back at five in the morning when he makes the donuts!"

June 25th

A traveling salesman checked into a futuristic motel. Realizing he needed a haircut before his next day's meeting, he called down to the desk clerk and asked if there was a barber on the premises.

"I'm afraid not, sir," the clerk told him apologetically, "but down the hall is a special machine that should serve your purposes."

Sceptical but intrigued, the salesman located the appropriate machine, inserted fifty pence, and stuck his head in the opening, at which time the machine started to buzz and whirl.

Fifteen seconds later the salesman pulled out his head and surveyed his head in the mirror, which reflected the best haircut he ever received in his life.

Down the hall was another machine with a sign that read, "Manicures - 25 pence."

"Why not," thought the salesman. He paid the money, inserted his hands into the slot, and pulled them out perfectly manicured.

The next machine had a huge sign that read, "This Machine Provides What Men Need Most When Away from Their Wives - cost 50 pence,"

The salesman was embarrassed and looked both ways. Seeing nobody around, he put in fifty pence, then unzipped his pants and stuck his willie into the opening - with great anticipation, since he had been away from his wife for 2 weeks.

When the machine started buzzing, the guy let out a shriek of agony.

Fifteen seconds later it shut off and, with trembling hands, the salesman withdrew his willie, complete with a button sewed on the tip.

June 26th

One day, the teacher walks into her classroom and announces to the class that on each Friday, she will ask a question to the class and anyone who answers correctly doesn't have to go to school the following Monday.

On the first Friday, the teacher asks, "How many grains of sand are in the beach?" Needless to say, no one could answer.

The following Friday, the teacher asks the class, "How many stars are in the sky?" and again no one could answer. Frustrated, little Johnny decides that the next Friday, he would somehow answer the question and get a 3 day weekend.

So Thursday night, Johnny takes two ping-pong balls and paints them black.

The next day, he brings them to school in a paper bag.

 At the end of the day, just when the teacher says, "Here's this week's question," Johnny empties the bag to the floor sending the ping-pong balls rolling to the front of the room.

Because they are young kids who find any disruption of class amusing, the entire class starts laughing.

The teacher says, "Okay, who's the comedian with the black balls?"

Immediately, little Johnny stands up and says, "Bill Cosby, see ya on Tuesday!"

June 27th

One day Holly's mother was out and her dad was in charge of her.

 Someone had given her a little 'tea set' as a gift. It was one of her favourite toys.

Daddy was in the living room engrossed in the evening news when she brought him a little cup of 'tea', which was just water.

After several cups of tea and lots of praise for such yummy tea, Holly's mum came home.

Her dad made her sit quietly in another room, so her mum could watch her bring dad the cup of tea, because she was so cute.

Mum waited, and sure enough, she came walking down the hall with a cup of tea for Daddy.

Mum watched dad drink from the tea cup.

Then she said, (as only a mother would know......)

'Did it ever occur to you that the only place she can reach to get water is the toilet?'

June 28th

There was a man who really took care of his body. He lifted weights and jogged 6 miles a day. One day, he took a look in the mirror and noticed that he was tanned all over except his willie. So, he decided to do something about it. He went to the beach, completely undressed himself and buried in the sand, except for his willie which he left sticking out.

Two old ladies were strolling along the beach, one using a cane. Upon seeing the willie sticking up over the sand, she began to move it around with her cane, remarking to the other lady, "There's no justice in the world."

The other lady asked what she meant.

When I was 20, I was curious about it.

When I was 30, I enjoyed it.

When I was 40, I asked for it.

When I was 50, I paid for it.

When I was 60, I prayed for it.

When I was 70, I forgot about it.

Now, I am 80 and the damn things are growing wild on the beach and I'm too old to squat."

☺☺

June 29th

A little boy and his grandfather are raking leaves in the yard. The little boy finds an earthworm trying to get back into its hole. He says, "Grandpa, I bet I can put that worm back in that hole." The grandfather replies, "I'll bet you five dollars you can't. It's too wiggly and limp to put back in that little hole."

The little boy runs into the house and comes back out with a can of hairspray. He sprays the worm until it is straight and stiff as a board. Then he puts the worm back into the hole.

The grandfather hands the little boy five dollars, grabs the hairspray, and runs into the house. Thirty minutes later the grandfather comes back out and hands the little boy another five dollars. The little boy says,

"Grandpa, you already gave me five dollars."

The grandfather replies, "I know. That's from your grandma."

☺☺

June 30th

Aging Mildred was a 93 year old woman who was particularly despondent over the recent death of her husband Earl. She decided that she would just kill herself and join him in death.

Thinking that it would be best to get it over with quickly, she took out Earl's old Army pistol and made the decision to shoot herself in the heart since it was so badly broken in the first place.

Not wanting to miss the vital organ and become a vegetable and a burden to someone, she called her doctor's office to inquire as to just exactly where the heart would be. "On a woman," the doctor said, "the heart would be just below the left breast."

Later that night, Mildred was admitted to the hospital with a gunshot wound to her knee.

"You might be an autism parent if modesty is an unknown entity and NOTHING seems to embarrass you anymore.'

Whenever we are out and about Rachel has to come into the toilet with me so that I can see to her toileting needs and also so I know she won't run off. I always see to her first and then use the toilet myself. We stopped at a very busy service station one day to use the facilities and these particular toilets had doors that opened outwards rather than inwards and had an easy sliding mechanism on the door for the lock. I had seen to Rachel and had just sat down to sort my own needs out when she opened the door wide for everyone to see. I couldn't stand up as I was 'mid-flow' and despite asking Rachel over and over to shut the door she ignored me, so I just had to grin and bear it until some kind woman pushed the door to for me.

On the caravan site there are approximately 600 caravans and one day I was walking with Rachel when she bolted from me and ran into another caravan. I had just had a hernia operation about 2 weeks previous and wasn't moving very quickly. There was a woman in the caravan cleaning it to get ready for her departure. Rachel rushed past her, signing toilet with one hand while pulling her shorts down with the other, sat down on the toilet, with the door wide open, and had a number two. Great!

Although she likes swimming, she doesn't like the feel of her wet swimsuits once she is out of the water, so it is always a mad dash back to the caravan to stop her from stripping off. One day we had just arrived back at the caravan when a holidaymaker stopped to talk to us. We had opened the door for Rachel and I was standing on the road talking with my back to the door. A few minutes later the poor man looked at me and said 'did you know your daughter is naked behind you?' I turned around and there was Rachel coming out of the door, totally naked, swinging her knickers in her hand, she was 19 years old at the time. If anyone wants to talk to us now and Rachel has a wet swimsuit on I make them wait a minute until she is changed.

July

July 1st

During camouflage training in Louisiana, a private disguised as a tree trunk had made a sudden move that was spotted by a visiting general.

"You simpleton!" the officer barked. "Don't you know that by jumping and yelling the way you did, you could have endangered the lives of the entire company?"

"Yes sir," the solder answered apologetically. "But, if I may say so, I did stand still when a flock of pigeons used me for target practice and I never moved a muscle when a large dog peed on my lower branches but when two squirrels ran up my pants leg and I heard the bigger say,

"Let's eat one now and save the other until winter' ---that did it."

July 2nd

On hearing that her elderly grandfather had just passed away, Katie went straight to her grandparent's house to visit her 95 year old grandmother and comfort her.

When she asked how her grandfather had died, her grandmother replied, "He had a heart attack while we were making love on Sunday morning."

Horrified, Katie told her grandmother that 2 people nearly 100 years old having sex would surely be asking for trouble.

"Oh no, my dear, "replied granny. "Many years ago, realizing our advanced age, we figured out the best time to do it was when the church bells would start to ring. It was just the right rhythm. Nice and slow and even. Nothing too strenuous, simply in on the ding and out on the dong."

She paused, wiped away a tear and then continued, "And if that damned ice cream truck hadn't come along, he'd still be alive today!"

July 3rd

A man and a woman were having drinks when they got into an argument about who enjoyed sex more.
The man said, "Men obviously enjoy sex more than women. Why do you think we're so obsessed with getting laid?"
"That doesn't prove anything," the woman countered.
"Think about this...when your ear itches and you put your finger in it and wiggle it around, then pull it out, which feels better-your ear or your finger?"

July 4th

A young woman buys a mirror at an antique shop and hangs it on her bathroom door. One evening, while getting undressed, she playfully says, "Mirror, mirror, on my door, make my bust-line forty-four."
Instantly, there is a brilliant flash of light, and her breasts grow to enormous proportions. Excitedly, she runs to tell her husband what happened, and in minutes they both return.
This time the husband crossed his fingers and says, "Mirror, mirror on the door, make my willie touch the floor."
Again, there is a bright flash and..........both his legs fall off.

July 5th

A woman and a baby were in the doctor's examining room, waiting for the doctor to come in for the baby's first exam. The doctor arrived, and examined the baby, checked his weight, and being a little concerned, asked if the baby was breast fed or bottle fed.

"Breast fed," she replied.

"Well, strip down to your waist," the doctor ordered. She did.

He pinched her nipples, pressed, kneaded, and rubbed both breasts for a while, in a very professional and detailed examination.

Motioning to her to get dressed, the doctor said, "No wonder this baby is underweight. You don't have any milk."

I know," she said, "I'm his Grandma, but I'm glad I came."

July 6th

Mary and Betty are twin sisters in St. Monica's Nursing Home. They were about to celebrate turning one hundred years old.

The editor of the local newspaper told a photographer to get over there and take pictures of the two 100 year old twins.

Mary was very deaf and Betty could not hear very well also.

Once the photographer arrived he asked the sisters to sit on the sofa.

Mary said to her twin, "What did he say?"

"We gotta sit over there on the sofa!" shouted Betty.

"Now get a little closer together," said the cameraman.

Mary asked, "What did he say?"

"He says we have to squeeze together a little." replied
Betty.
So they wiggled up close to each other. "Just hold on for a
bit longer,
I've got to FOCUS a little," said the photographer.
Mary again said, "What did he say?" Betty replied.....
"He said he's going to FOCUS!"
With a big grin Mary shouted out, "Wow - Both of us?"

July 7th

"A woman just gave birth to a baby in hospital. As soon as
she had recovered the doctor came to speak to her.
"Your baby is in good health, but there is something I need
to tell you...."
The woman became worried..."What's the matter...Please
tell me, what's wrong with my baby?"
"There's nothing wrong, it's just that your baby is a little
different. He is a Hermaphrodite."
"HERMAPHRODITE.....What's that?"
"Well.....it means your baby is.....that your baby has all the
equipment of a man but also of a lady"
The woman pales then say's........
"OH MY GOD......you mean...... he has ....
A WILLY and a BRAIN!!!!!!!

July 8th

Mr. Smith goes to the doctor's office to collect his wife's
test results.
The lab tech says to him, "I'm sorry, sir, but there has been
a bit of a mix-up and we have a problem. When we sent

the samples from your wife to the lab, the samples from another Mrs Smith were sent as well and we are now uncertain which one is your wife's.
 Frankly, that's either bad or terrible."
"What do you mean?"
"Well, one Mrs. Smith has tested positive for Alzheimer's disease and the other for AIDS. We can't tell which one is your wife's."
"That's terrible! Can we do the test over?" asked Mr. Smith.
"Normally, yes, but the NHS won't pay for these expensive tests more than once."
"Well, what am I supposed to do now?"
"The NHS recommends that you drop your wife off in the middle of town. If she finds her way home, don't sleep with her."

July 9th
"You're in remarkable shape for a man your age," said the doctor to the ninety-year old man after the examination.
"I know it," said the old gentleman. "I've really got only one complaint-my sex drive is too high. Got anything you can do for that, Doc?"
The doctor's mouth dropped open. "Your what?!" he gasped.
"My sex drive," said the old man. "It's too high, and I'd like to have you lower it if you can."
"Lower it?!" exclaimed the doctor, still unable to believe what the ninety-year old gentleman was saying. "Just what do you consider 'high'?"

"These days it seems like it's all in my head, Doc," said the old man, "and I'd like to have you lower it a couple of feet if you can."

July 10th

A new wine has been developed for seniors.
A single glass at night could mean a peaceful, uninterrupted night's sleep.
Clare Valley vintners in South Australia, which primarily produce Pinot Blanc, Pinot Noir, and Pinot Grigio wines, have developed a new hybrid grape that acts as an anti-diuretic.
It is expected to reduce the number of trips older people have to make to the bathroom during the night.
The new wine will be marketed as: PINO MORE

July 11th

A man returns from the doctor and tells his wife that the doctor has told him he has only 24 hours to live.
Given this prognosis, the man asks his wife for sex.
Naturally, she agrees, and they make love.
About six hours later, the husband goes to his wife and says, "Honey, you know I now have only 18 hours to live. Could we please do it one more time?"
Of course, the wife agrees, and they do it again.
 Later, as the man gets into bed, he looks at his watch and realizes that he now has only 8 hours left. He touches his wife shoulder, and asks, "Honey, please...just one more time before die."

She says, "Of course, Dear," and they make love for the third time.

After this session, the wife rolls over and falls asleep.

The man, however, worried about his impending death, tosses and turns, until he's down to 4 more hours. He taps his wife, who rouses. "Honey, I have only 4 more hours. Do you think we could...?"

At this point the wife sits up and says, "Listen, I have to get up in the morning. You don't!"

July 12th

A little girl asked her Mum, "Mum, may I take the dog for a walk around the block?"

Mum replies "No, because she is in heat."

"What's that mean?" asked the child.

"Go ask your father", answered the mother, "I think he's in the garage."

The little girl goes to the garage and says, "Dad, may I take Belle for a walk around the block? I asked Mum, but she said the dog was in heat, and to come to you."

Dad said, "Bring Belle over here." He took a rag, soaked it with gasoline, and scrubbed the dog's backside with it and said, "Okay, you can go now, but keep Belle on the leash and only go one time around the block."

The little girl left, and returned a few minutes later with no dog on the leash. Surprised, Dad asked, "Where's Belle?"

The little girl said, "She ran out of gas about halfway down the block, so another dog is pushing her home."

July 13th

A tour bus driver is driving a bus load of OAPs on a day-trip when he is tapped on his shoulder by a little old lady. She offers him a handful of peanuts, which he gratefully munches up.

After about 15 minutes, she taps him on the shoulder again and gives him another handful of peanuts.

She repeats this gesture about five more times.

As she is about to hand him yet another batch, he asks the little old lady, 'Why don't you eat the peanuts yourself?'

She replies: `None of us can chew them because we have no teeth'.

The puzzled driver asks, 'So why do you buy them then?'

She replied, 'Oh, we just love the chocolate around them.'

July 14th

A cardiac specialist died and at his funeral the coffin was placed in front of a huge mock-up of a heart made up of flowers. When the pastor finished with the sermon and eulogy, and after everyone said their good-byes, the heart opened, the coffin rolled inside and the heart closed. Just then one of the mourners burst into laughter.

The guy next to him asked: "Why are you laughing?"

"I was thinking about my own funeral," the man replied.

"What's so funny about that?"

"I'm a gynaecologist."

July 15th

A lady goes to the doctor and complains her husband is losing interest in sex.

He gives her a pill but warns her that it's still experimental. He tells her to slip it in his mashed potatoes at dinner. At dinner that night, she does just that.

About a week later she's back at the doctor and tells him, "The pill worked great! I put it in his mashed potatoes like you said.

It wasn't five minutes later that he jumped up, pushed all the food and dishes to the floor, grabbed me, ripped off all my clothes and ravaged me right there on the table."

The doctor says, "Oh dear -- I'm sorry, we didn't realize the pill was that strong. The foundation will be glad to pay for any damages."

The lady replied, "That's very kind - but I don't think the restaurant will let us back in anyway."

July 16th

A kilted Scotsman was walking down a country path after finishing off a large amount of whisky at a local pub. He felt quite sleepy and decided to nap against a tree.

As he slept, two female tourists heard his loud snoring. When they found him, one said, "I've always wondered what a Scotsman wears under his kilt."

She boldly walked over to the sleeper, raised his kilt, and saw that he wore nothing at all. Her friend said, "Well, the mystery is solved! Let's thank him for sharing!"

She took off her pretty blue hair ribbon and gently tied it around the Scotsman's willy.

A little while later, the Scotsman was awakened by the call of nature.

He raised his kilt and was bewildered at the sight of the neatly tied blue ribbon.

He stared for a minute, then said, "I don't know where y'been laddie... but it's nice ta see you won firrrst prrrize!"

☺☺

July 17th
A biker goes to the doctor with hearing problems. "Can you describe the symptoms to me?" asked the doctor.
 "Yes. Homer is a fat yellow lazy fella and Marge is a skinny bird with big blue hair."

☺☺

July 18th
A group of kindergartners were trying to become accustomed to the first grade. The biggest hurdle they faced was that the teacher insisted on no baby talk.
"You need to use 'big people' words," she'd always remind them. She asked Chris what he had done over the weekend. "I went to visit my Nana" he said.
"No, you went to visit your GRANDMOTHER. Use 'big people' words!"
She then asked Mitchell what he had done. "I took a ride on a choo-choo."
She said, "No, you took a ride on a TRAIN. Use 'big people' words!" She then asked Bobby what he had done. "I read a book," he replied.
"That's WONDERFUL!" the teacher said. "What book did you read?" Bobby thought about it, then puffed out his little chest with great pride and said, "Winnie the Shit."

July 19th

A husband and wife are trying to set up a new password for their computer.

The husband puts, "Mypenis," and the wife falls on the ground laughing because on the screen it says, "Error. Not long enough."

July 20th

There once was a religious young woman who went to Confession. Upon entering the confessional, she said, 'Forgive me, Father, for I have sinned.'

The priest said, ' Confess your sins and be forgiven.'

The young woman said, 'Last night my boyfriend made mad passionate love to me seven times.'

The priest thought long and hard and then said, 'Squeeze seven lemons into a glass and then drink the juice.'

The young woman asked, 'Will this cleanse me of my sins?'

The priest said, 'No, but it will wipe that smile off of your face.'

July 21st

A guy walks into a bathroom, sits down, and notices three buttons in front of him marked, WW, WA, and ATR.

Curiosity gets the better of him so he decides to press WW.

Suddenly, warm water sprays up his rear. "Mmmm," he says to himself. "That was good." so he presses WA and a jet of warm air dries his backside.

"Mmmm. Nice!" So finally he can't resist pressing the ATR button.

The next thing he knows, he is waking up in a hospital ward just as the nurse is entering the room.

"Nurse, Nurse! Where am I? What happened?"

The nurse replies, "You must have missed the sign to not press the ATR button."

"What does ATR mean exactly?" says the guy.

"Automatic Tampon Remover. Your testicles are under your pillow."

July 22nd

A circus owner walked into a bar to see everyone crowded about a table watching a little show. On the table was an upside down pot and a duck tap dancing on it. The circus owner was so impressed that he offered to buy the duck from its owner.

After some wheeling and dealing, they settled for £10,000 for the duck and the pot.

Three days later the circus owner runs back to the bar in anger, "Your duck is a rip-off! I put him on the pot before a whole audience, and he didn't dance a single step!"

"So?" asked the ducks former owner, "did you remember to light the candle under the pot?"

July 23rd

A man stumbles up to the only other patron in a bar and asks if he could buy him a drink. "Why of course," comes the reply.

The first man then asks: "Where are you from?"

"I'm from Ireland," replies the second man.

The first man responds: "You don't say, I'm from Ireland too! Let's have another round to Ireland."

"Of course," replies the second man.

I'm curious, the first man then asks: "Where in Ireland are you from?"

"Dublin," comes the reply.

"I can't believe it," says the first man. "I'm from Dublin too! Let's have another drink to Dublin."

"Of course," replies the second man.

Curiosity again strikes and the first man asks: "What school did you go to?"

"Saint Mary's," replies the second man, "I graduated in '62."

"This is unbelievable!", the first man says. "I went to Saint Mary's and I graduated in '62, too!"

About that time in comes one of the regulars and sits down at the bar. "What's been going on?" he asks the bartender.

"Nothing much," replies the bartender. "The O'Kelly twins are drunk again."

July 24th

A man walks into a bar and asks the bartender, "If I show you a really good trick, will you give me a free drink?"

The bartender considers it, then agrees. The man reaches into his pocket and pulls out a tiny rat. He reaches into his other pocket and pulls out a tiny piano. The rat stretches, cracks his knuckles, and proceeds to play the blues.

After the man finished his drink, he asked the bartender, "If I show you an even better trick, will you give me free drinks for the rest of the evening?"

The bartender agrees, thinking that no trick could possibly be better than the first.

The man reaches into another pocket and pulls out a small bullfrog who begins to sing along with the rat's music. While the man is enjoying his beverages, a stranger confronts him and offers him £100,000.00 for the bullfrog. "Sorry," the man replies, "he's not for sale."

The stranger increases the offer to £250,000.00 cash up front. "No," he insists, "he's not for sale."

The stranger again increases the offer, this time to £500,000.00 cash. The man finally agrees, and turns the frog over to the stranger in exchange for the money.

"Are you insane?" the bartender demanded. "That frog could have been worth millions to you, and you let him go for a mere £500,000!" "Don't worry about it." the man answered. "The frog was really nothing special. You see, the rat's a ventriloquist."

July 25th

A businessman enters a pub, sits down at the bar, and orders a double martini on the rocks. After he finishes the drink, he peeks inside his shirt pocket, and then he asks the bartender to prepare another double martini.

After he finishes that one, he again peeks inside his shirt pocket and asks the bartender to bring another double martini.

The bartender says, "Look, buddy, I'll bring ya' martinis all night long. But you gotta tell me why you look inside your shirt pocket before you order a refill."

The man replies, "I'm peeking at a photo of my wife. When she starts to look good, then I know it's time to go home."

☺☺

July 26th
A man in the Florida supermarket tries to buy half a head of lettuce.
The very young produce assistant tells him that they sell only whole heads of lettuce. The man persists and asks to see the manager. The boy says he'll ask his manager about it.
Walking into the back room, the boy said to his manager, "Some asshole wants to buy half a head of lettuce."
As he finished his sentence, he turned to find the man standing right behind him, so he added, "And this gentleman has kindly offered to buy the other half."
The manager approved the deal, and the man went on his way.
Later the manager said to the boy, "I was impressed with the way you got yourself out of that situation earlier. We like people who think on their feet here. Where are you from, son?"
"Canada, sir," the boy replied.
"Well, why did you leave Canada?" the manager asked.
The boy said, "Sir, there's nothing but whores and hockey players up there."
"Really?" said the manager. "My wife is from Canada."
"Is that right" replied the boy. "Who'd she play for?"

July 27th
A little girl and boy are fighting about the differences between the sexes, and which one is better.
 Finally, the boy drops his pants and says, "Here's something I have that you'll never have!"

The little girl is pretty upset by this, since it is clearly true, and runs home crying.

A little while later, she comes running back with a smile on her face.

She drops her pants and says, "My mummy says that with one of these, I can have as many of those as I want!"

July 28th

Every ten years, the monks in the monastery are allowed to break their vow of silence to speak two words.

Ten years go by and it's one monk's first chance. He thinks for a second before saying, "Food bad."

Ten years later, he says, "Bed hard."

It's the big day, a decade later. He gives the head monk a long stare and says, "I quit."

"I'm not surprised," the head monk says. "You've been complaining ever since you got here."

July 29th

A blind man with a Seeing Eye dog at his side walks into a grocery store. The man walks to the middle of the store, picks up the dog by the tail, and starts swinging the dog around in circles over his head.

The store manager, who has seen all this, thinks this is quite strange. So, he decides to find out what's going on. The store manager approaches the blind man swinging the dog and says, "Pardon me. May I help you with something?"

The blind man says, "No thanks. I'm just looking around."

☺☺

July 30th
Cinderella is now 101 years old.
After a fulfilling life with the now dead prince, she happily
sits upon her rocking chair, watching the world go by from
her front porch, with a cat named Bob for companionship.
One sunny afternoon out of nowhere, appeared the fairy
godmother. Cinderella said, 'Fairy Godmother, what are
you doing here after all these years'?
The fairy godmother replied, 'Cinderella, you have lived an
exemplary life since I last saw you. Is there anything for
which your heart still yearns?'
Cinderella was taken aback, overjoyed, and after some
thoughtful consideration, she uttered her first wish: 'The
prince was wonderful, but not much of an investor. I'm
living hand to mouth on my disability cheques, and I wish I
were wealthy beyond comprehension. Instantly her
rocking chair turned into solid gold. Cinderella said, 'Ooh,
thank you, Fairy Godmother'
The fairy godmother replied, 'It is the least that I can do.
What do you want for your second wish?' Cinderella
looked down at her frail body, and said,
'I wish I were young and full of the beauty and youth I
once had.' At once, her wish became reality, and her
beautiful young visage returned. Cinderella felt stirrings
inside her that had been dormant for years.
And then the fairy godmother spoke once more: 'You have
one more wish; what shall it be?'
 Cinderella looks over to the frightened cat in the corner
and says, 'I wish for you to transform Bob, my old cat, into
a kind and handsome young man.' Magically, Bob
suddenly underwent so fundamental a change in his
biological make-up that, when he stood before her, he was

a man so beautiful the likes of him neither she nor the world had ever seen.

The fairy godmother said, 'Congratulations, Cinderella, enjoy your new life.'

With a blazing shock of bright blue electricity, the fairy godmother was gone as suddenly as she appeared.

For a few eerie moments, Bob and Cinderella looked into each other's eyes. Cinderella sat, breathless, gazing at the most beautiful, stunningly perfect man she had ever seen.

Then Bob walked over to Cinderella, who sat transfixed in her rocking chair, and held her close in his young muscular arms.

He leaned in close, blowing her golden hair with his warm breath as he whispered...

'Bet you're sorry you had me castrated now aren't you?'

July 31st

An elderly couple had dinner at another couple's house, and after eating, the wives left the table and went into the kitchen.

The two gentlemen were talking, and one said, "Last night we went out to a new restaurant and it was really great. I would recommend it very highly."

The other man said, "What is the name of the restaurant?"

The first man thought and thought and finally said, "What is the name of that flower you give to someone you love? You know... the one that's red and has thorns."

"Do you mean a rose?"

"Yes, that's the one," replied the man.

He then turned towards the kitchen and yelled, "Rose, what's the name of that restaurant we went to last night?"

☺☺

"You might be an autism parent if you've ever had toys thrown at your head while driving because you dared to go a different way and you can't drive with the window down in case your child throws something out of the window.'

This was a phase Rachel went through when she was young for a short while, and one which she thankfully outgrew very quickly.

One day my mum had come to pick Rachel up to look after her for the afternoon and decided to drive a different way home than normal. Rachel couldn't comprehend the different direction, she had a couple of video cassettes in her hand and hit mum over the back of the head with one when she stopped at a roundabout and then threw it out of the window. She was never allowed her videos in the back seat of mum's car again and she was always made to sit in the rear passenger side seat where she couldn't reach my mum when she was driving.

One day we were driving on the motorway in France being followed by our friends in the car behind. Rachel had one of those small plastic tennis bats with the ball attached on an elastic band. She suddenly opened the window and threw it out hitting our friend's windscreen at 80mph. The windscreen didn't break, but our friend said he needed to change his underwear it made such a loud bang.

August

August 1st

Two Buddies were drinking in a bar one night and had become extremely drunk. One guy was so drunk that he had got sick all over his shirt. He looks at his buddy and says "My wife is going to kill me when I get home; this is a brand new shirt!

His buddy looks at him and says "don't worry, just put $20 in your front pocket and tell her that some guy got sick on you and gave you $20 for the cleaning bill.

The guy thinks this is an excellent idea and continues to drink. After a while he heads home. When he arrives and opens the front door his wife is standing there waiting on him.

"Just look at you, you drunken bugger! You've got sick all over yourself".

The man replies "No baby, it isn't like that some guy got sick on me and look here he gave me $20 for the cleaning bill.

She pulls the money out of his pocket and counts it and says "Wait one minute there's $40 here!

The guy looks at her and says "Oh yea, he shit in my pants too!"

August 2nd

Three women, two younger, and one senior citizen, were sitting naked in a sauna.

Suddenly there was a beeping sound. The young woman pressed her forearm and the beeping stopped.

The others looked at her questioningly. 'That was my pager,' she said; I have a microchip under the skin of my arm.

A few minutes later, a phone rang. The second young woman lifted her palm to her ear. When she finished, she explained, 'That was my mobile phone. I have a microchip in my hand.'

The older woman felt very low -tech. Not to be out done, she decided she had to do something just as impressive. She stepped out of the sauna and went to the bathroom. She returned with a piece of toilet paper hanging from her rear end.

The others raised their eyebrows and stared at her.

The older woman finally said........"well, will you look at that... I'm getting a fax!!"

August 3rd

A Minister, a Priest, and a Rabbi are talking shop one day, and the discussion turns to how they divide up the donated money that their congregations give at their respective services to the collection plate. Specifically, how much goes to maintaining the infrastructure, and how much does the Minister/Priest/Rabbi keep to live on.

The Minister explains that that she draws a circle on the ground, and tosses the money up in the air. Whatever falls inside the circle is for her to support herself and family on, and whatever falls outside is God's, that is - for the Church and its various programs.

The Priest nods knowingly, and says that he has a very similar system - except that in his case whatever money falls inside the circle is God's, and whatever falls outside is his living allowance.

The Rabbi nods, and says that his system is also similar, except it doesn't involve a drawing circle. The Priest and Minister look at him quizzically, and ask him to go on....

The Rabbi continues "I throw all the money up in the air - - Whatever God wants, he keeps...."

August 4th

A refuse collector is going along a street picking up the wheelie bins and emptying them into his dustcart.

He goes to one house where the bin hasn't been left out, so he has a quick look for it, goes round the back of the house, but still can't see it.

So, against the rules of the refuse collector's code but in the spirit of kindness, he knocks on the door.

There's no answer.

Being a kindly and conscientious bloke, he knocks again - much harder.

Eventually a Japanese bloke comes to the door.

"Harro!" says the Japanese chappie.

"Gidday, mate! Where's ya bin?" asks the collector

"I bin on toiret" explains the Japanese bloke, a bit perplexed.

Realising the little foreign fellow had misunderstood him, the bin man smiles and tries again...

"No mate, where's your dust bin?".

"I dust been to toiret, I toll you!'" says the Japanese man - still perplexed.

"Listen," says the collector.

"You're misunderstanding me. Where's your w h e e l i e bin?"

"Ok. Ok " replies the Japanese man with a sheepish grin.

" I wheelie bin havin sex wirra wife's sister........!"

August 5th

A farmer walks into his bedroom carrying a lamb under his arm. He walks over to his wife who's lying in bed.

"See!" he yells, "This is the pig I have to have sex with whenever you get one of your headaches!"

The wife says, "You know that's a lamb under your arm, don't you?"

The farmer says, "I wasn't talking to you."

August 6th

Once upon a time there were two brothers. One brother was very mischievous, always getting into trouble.

The other brother, however, was very good. He was always kind to animals, helped elderly neighbours, and led an exemplary life......

As time went on, the brothers stayed in touch but were never close.

The evil brother became a heavy drinker and a womanizer. The other brother was a devoted husband and father and supported many charities.

One day the evil brother died and then after a few years, the good brother passed away as well.

He went to heaven and was rewarded with a happy and eternal afterlife.

One day he went to God and asked, "Where is my brother? He died before me, but I have not seen him here in heaven.."

God replied, "As you know, your brother led an evil life so he is not spending eternity here in heaven. He has been sent elsewhere."

"I'm sorry to hear that", the good brother replied. "But I do miss him and wish I could see him again.

"You can see him if you wish", God said, "I will give you power to gaze into hell."

So the power was granted and the good brother gazed into hell.

Before long he saw his brother sitting on a bench.

In one arm he held a keg of beer, and in the other he cradled a gorgeous young blonde.

The good brother turned to God and said, "I can't believe what I'm seeing.

I have found my brother, and he has a keg of beer in one arm and a beautiful woman in the other. Surely, hell can't be that bad."

God explained. "Things are not always as they seem my son, the keg has a hole in it and the blonde doesn't."

August 7th

Three Kiwis and three Aussies are traveling by train to a conference.

At the station, the three Aussies each buy tickets and watch as the three Kiwis buy only a single ticket.

"How are three people going to travel on only one ticket?" asks an Aussie.

"Watch and you'll see," answers a Kiwi.

They all board the train. The Aussies take their respective seats but all three Kiwis cram into a bathroom and close the door behind them.

Shortly after the train has departed, the conductor comes around collecting tickets. He knocks on the bathroom door and says, "Ticket, please." The door opens just a crack and a single arm emerges with a ticket in hand. The conductor takes it and moves on.

The Aussies see this and agree it was quite a clever idea. So after the conference, the Aussies decide to copy the Kiwis on the return trip and save some money (being clever with money, and all that).

When they get to the station, they buy a single ticket for the return trip.

To their astonishment, the Kiwis don't buy a ticket at all.

"How are you going to travel without a ticket?" says one perplexed Aussie.

Watch and you'll see," answers a kiwi.

When they board the train the three Aussies cram into a bathroom and the three Kiwis cram into another one nearby and the train departs.

Shortly afterward, one of the Kiwis leaves his bathroom and walks over to the bathroom where the Aussies are hiding.

He knocks on the door and says, "Ticket, please."

August 8th

An Aussie journalist was in New Zealand doing stories where he saw a Kiwi farmer doing unnatural things with a sheep.

He approached the Kiwi and firstly asked, "What sort of sheep is that?"

He scribbled down the farmer's reply - "a Merino".

The next question was, "Do you shear them?"

The farmer replied hastily, "No! Go and find yer own!"

August 9th

It was many years ago since the embarrassing day when a young woman, with a baby in her arms, entered his butcher shop and confronted the butcher with the news that the baby was his and asked what was he going to do about it?

Finally he offered to provide her with free meat until the boy was 16. She agreed.

He had been counting the years off on his calendar, and one day the teenager who had been collecting the meat each week, came into the shop and said, "I'll be 16 tomorrow."

"I know," said the butcher with a smile, "I've been counting too, tell your mother, when you take this parcel of meat home, that it is the last free meat she'll get, and watch the expression on her face."

When the boy arrived home he told his mother. The woman nodded and said, "Son, go back to the butcher and tell him I have also had free bread, free milk, and free groceries for the last 16 years and watch the expression on HIS face!"

August 10th

Three little boys at school have an argument on who had the coolest dad in school.

The first little boy said "My Dad's pretty cool, "ya know because he can do smoke rings one after the other straight outta his mouth."

The second little boy replied "Oh, yeah but my Dad can do exactly the same but outta his nose, cool ah?"

The third little boy said both your dads are absolute nerds because my Dad can do smoke rings but guess where from?....His bum"
The first two boys were pretty impressed but replied "Oh yeah sure, have you seen him do 'em?"
The third boy replied "No, but I sure have seen the nicotine stains on his undies."

☺☺

August 11th

One day a cynical husband asked why his wife was so bright and cheerful.
"I saw my doctor today and he said I had firm breasts like an 18 year old"
"Yes," said the husband, "but what did he say about your 45 year old arse?"
"Your name wasn't mentioned." she said.

☺☺

August 12th

There once was a farmer who was raising 3 daughters on his own. He was very concerned about their wellbeing and always did his best to watch out for them. As they entered their late teens the girls dated, and on this particular evening all three of his girls were going out on a date. This was the first time this had occurred. As was his custom, he would greet the young suitor at the door holding his shotgun, not to menace or threaten but merely to ensure that the young man knew who was boss.
The doorbell rang and the first of the boys arrived.

Father answered the door and the lad said, "Hi, my name's Joe, I'm here for Flo. We're going to the show, is she ready to go?"

The father looked him over and sent the kids on their way.

The next lad arrived and said, "My name's Eddie, I'm here for Betty, we're gonna get some spaghetti, is she ready?"

Father felt this one was okay too, so off the two kids went.

The final young man arrived and the farmer opened the door. The boy started off, "Hi, my name's Chuck..." the farmer shot him.

August 13th

A man was leaving a cafe with his morning coffee when he noticed a most unusual funeral procession approaching the nearby cemetery. A long black hearse was followed by a second long black hearse about 20 yards behind the first. Behind the second hearse was a solitary man walking a pit-bull on a leash. Behind him was a queue of 200 men walking in single file.

The man couldn't stand the curiosity. He respectfully approached the man walking the dog.

"I am so sorry for your loss, and I know now is a bad time to disturb you, but I've never seen a funeral like this with so many of you walking in single file. Whose funeral is it?"

The man replied, "Well, the first hearse is for my wife."

"What happened to her?"

The man replied, "My dog attacked and killed her."

He inquired further, "Well, who is in the second hearse?"

The man answered, "My mother-in-law. She was trying to help my wife when the dog turned on her."

A poignant and thoughtful moment of silence passes between the two men.
"Can I borrow the dog?"
"Join the queue."

August 14th

An 86-year-old man went to his doctor for his quarterly check-up...

The doctor asked him how he was feeling, and the 86-year-old said, "Things are great and I've never felt better. I now have a 20 year-old bride who is pregnant with my child. So what do you think about that Doc?"

The doctor considered his question for a minute and then began to tell a story.

"I have an older friend, much like you, who is an avid hunter and never misses a season. One day he was setting off to go hunting. In a bit of a hurry, he accidentally picked up his walking cane instead of his gun."

"As he neared a lake, he came across a very large male beaver sitting at the water's edge. He realized he'd left his gun at home and so he couldn't shoot the magnificent creature. Out of habit he raised his cane, aimed it at the animal as if it were his favourite hunting rifle and went 'bang, bang'."

"Miraculously, two shots rang out and the beaver fell over dead. Now, what do you think of that?" asked the doctor.

The 86-year-old said, "Logic would strongly suggest that somebody else pumped a couple of rounds into that beaver."

The doctor replied, "My point exactly."

August 15th

A Mafia Godfather, accompanied by his attorney, walks into a room to meet with his former accountant.

The Godfather asks the accountant, "Where is the 3 million bucks you embezzled from me?" The accountant does not answer.

The Godfather asks again, "Where is the 3 million bucks you embezzled from me?"

The attorney interrupts, "Sir, the man is a deaf mute and cannot understand you, but I can interpret for you."

The Godfather says, "Well ask him where my damn money is!" The attorney, using sign language, asks the accountant where the 3 million dollars is.

The accountant signs back, "I don't know what you are talking about."

The attorney interprets to the Godfather, "He doesn't know what you are talking about."

The Godfather pulls out a 9 millimetre pistol, puts it to the temple of the accountant, cocks the trigger and says, "Ask him again where my damn money is!"

The attorney signs to the accountant, "He wants to know where it is!"

The accountant signs back, "OK! OK! OK! The money is hidden in a brown suitcase behind the shed in my backyard!"

The Godfather says, "Well....what did he say?"

The attorney interprets to the Godfather, "He says...go to hell......and you don't have the guts to pull the trigger."

August 16th

A Polish immigrant went to the DLVA to apply for a driver's license.

First, of course, he had to take an eye sight test.
The optician showed him a card with the letters......
'C Z W I X N O S T A C Z.'
'Can you read this?' the optician asked.
'Read it?' the Polish guy replied, 'I know the guy.'

August 17th

A Primary Teacher explains to her class that she is a MUFC fan.
She asks her students to raise their hands if they too are MUFC fans.
Everyone in the class raises their hand except one little girl..
The teacher looks at the girl with surprise and says, 'Mary, why didn't you raise your hand?'
'Because I'm not a MUFC fan,' she replied.
The teacher, still shocked, asked, 'Well, if you are not a MUFC fan, then who are you a fan of?'
'I am a Bolton fan, and proud of it,' Mary replied.
The teacher could not believe her ears. 'Mary, why, pray tell, are you a Bolton fan?'
'Because my mum is a Bolton fan, and my dad is a Bolton fan, so I'm a Bolton fan too!'
'Well,' said the teacher in an obviously annoyed tone, 'that is no reason for you to be a Bolton fan.
You don't have to be just like your parents all of the time...
What if your mum was a prostitute and your dad was a drug addict, what would you be then?'

'Then,' Mary smiled, 'I'd be a MUFC fan.

☺☺

August 18th

Three old ladies were sitting side by side in their retirement home reminiscing.

The first lady recalled shopping at the green grocers and demonstrated with her hands, the length and thickness of a cucumber she could buy for a penny.

The second old lady nodded, adding that onions used to be much bigger and cheaper also, and demonstrated the size of two big onions she could buy for a penny a piece..

The third old lady remarked, "I can't hear a word you're saying, but I remember the guy you're talking about."

August 19th

At the end of the tax year, the Revenue Office sent an inspector to audit the books of a local hospital.

While the agent was checking the books, he turned to the executive of the hospital and said "I notice you buy a lot of bandages. What do you do with the end of the roll when there's too little left to be of any use?"

"Good question," noted the executive. "We save them up and send them back to the bandage company and every once in a while, they send us a free roll."

"Oh," replied the auditor, somewhat disappointed that his unusual question had a practical answer.

But on he went, in his obnoxious way.

"What about all these plaster purchases? What do you do with what's left over after setting a cast on a patient?"

"Ah, yes," replied the executive, realizing that the inspector was trying to trap him with an unanswerable question. "We save it and send it back to the manufacturer and every so often they send us a free bag of plaster."

"I see," replied the auditor, thinking hard about how he could fluster the know-it-all executive. "Well, what do you do with all the remains from the circumcision surgeries?" "Here, too, we do not waste," answered the executive. "What we do is save all the little foreskins and send them to the tax office, and about once a year they send us a complete prick."

August 20th

August 20th

The largest condom factory in the States burned down. President Obama was awakened at 4 am by the telephone. "Sorry to bother you at this hour, Sir, but there is an emergency! I've just received word that the Durex factory in Washington has burned to the ground. It is estimated that the entire USA supply of condoms will be used up by the end of the week."
Obama: "Oh damn! The economy will never be able to cope with all those unwanted babies. We'll be ruined. We'll have to ship some in from Mexico."
Telephone voice says, "Bad idea... The Mexicans will have a field day with this one. We'll be a laughing stock. What about the UK?"
Obama: "Okay, I'll call Cameron and tell him we need five million condoms, ten inches long and three inches thick. That way, they'll continue to respect us as Americans."
Three days later, a delighted President Obama ran out to open the first of the 10,000 boxes that had just arrived. He found it full of condoms, 10 inches long and 3 inches thick, exactly as requested... All coloured with Union Jacks with small writing on each one:

MADE IN ENGLAND - SIZE: SMALL

☺☺

August 21st
A man is preparing to board a plane, when he hears that the Pope is on the same flight.

"This is great" thinks the man. "Perhaps I'll be able to see the pontiff in person"

Imagine his surprise when the Pope sits down in the seat next to him.

Shortly after take-off, the Pope begins a crossword puzzle. Almost immediately, the Pope turns to the man and says, "Excuse me, but do you know a four letter word referring to a woman that ends in `unt ?

Only one word leaps to mind. "Bugger me thinks the man, "I can't tell the Pope that.

There must be another word." The gentleman thinks for quite a while, and then it hits him.

Turning to the Pope, the man says, "I think the word you're looking for is aunt"

"Of course," says the Pope. "Do you have an eraser?"

August 22nd
On the morning that Daylight Savings Time ended I stopped in to visit my ageing friend.

He was busy covering his penis with black shoe polish.

I said to him, "You better get your hearing checked - You're supposed to turn your clock back".

August 23rd
Earl and Bubba are quietly sitting in a boat fishing, chewing tobacco and drinking beer when suddenly Bubba says, "Think I'm gonna divorce the wife – she ain't spoke to me in over 2 months."
Earl spits overboard, takes a long, slow sip of beer and says, "Better think it over ...women like that are hard to find."

August 24th
What did the blonde say when she saw the Cheerios box?

"Omg, donut seeds!"

August 25th
A group of seniors were sitting around talking about all their ailments at Costa Coffee.
"My arms have got so weak I can hardly lift this cup of coffee," said one.
"Yes, I know," said another. "My cataracts are so bad; I can't even see my coffee."
"I couldn't even mark an "X" at election time because my hands are so crippled," volunteered a third.
"What? Speak up! What? I can't hear you, said one elderly lady!"
"I can't turn my head because of the arthritis in my neck, "said one, to which several nodded weakly in agreement.
"My blood pressure pills make me so dizzy!" exclaimed another.
"I forget where I am, and where I'm going," said another.

"I guess that's the price we pay for getting old, "winced an old man as he slowly shook his head.
The others nodded in agreement.
"Well, count your Blessings," said a woman cheerfully....
"Thank God we can all still drive."

August 26th

Patrick and Murphy are talking over a pint of Guinness at their local bar.
Patrick said to Murphy "A strange thing happened at home last night"
Murphy inquired "And what was that"
Patrick answered "The wife asked me what I was doing on the computer"
Murphy - "And what did you tell her"
Patrick - "I told her I was looking for cheap flights"
Murphy - "So what did she say about that"
Patrick - "She said she loved me, threw me on the floor and we had the most amazing sex"
Murphy - "I'll bet that surprised you Pat"
Patrick - "That it did Murphy, she's never shown the remotest interest in darts before!"

August 27th

A flat-chested young lady went to Dr Smith about enlarging her tiny breasts.
Dr Smith advised her, 'Every day after your shower, rub your chest and say, 'Scooby doobie doobies, I want bigger boobies!'
She did this faithfully for several months!

She grew terrific D-cup boobs! One morning she was running late, got on the bus, and in a panic realized she had forgotten her morning ritual.

Frightened she might lose her lovely boobs if she didn't recite the little rhyme, she stood right there in the middle aisle of the bus closed her eyes and said, 'Scooby doobie doobies, I want bigger boobies.'

A guy sitting nearby looked at her and asked 'Oh! Are you a patient of Dr Smith's?'

'Yes I am. How did you know?'

He, winked and whispered, 'Hickory dickory dock...'

August 28th

Tired of constant blonde jokes, a blonde dyes her hair brown. She then goes for a drive in the country and sees a shepherd herding his sheep across the road.

"Hey, shepherd, if I guess how many sheep are here, can I keep one?"

The shepherd is puzzled but agrees. She blurts out "352!" He is stunned but keeps his word and allows her to pick a sheep.

"I'll take this one," she says proudly. "It's the cutest!"

"Hey lady," says the shepherd, "If I guess your real hair colour, can I have my dog back?"

August 29th

A farmer named Hank had 5 female pigs.

Times were hard, so Hank decided to take them to the county fair and sell them.

At the fair, he met another farmer who owned 5 male pigs. After talking a bit, they decided to mate the pigs and split everything 50/50. The farmers lived sixty miles apart, so they agreed to drive thirty miles each and find a field in which to let the pigs mate.

The first morning, Hank was up at 5 am with his female pigs, loaded them into the truck, and drove the thirty miles to their meeting place. While the pigs were mating, he asked the other farmer, "How will I know if my pigs are pregnant?"

The other farmer replied, "Simple Hank. If they're lying in the grass in the morning, they're pregnant; if they're in the mud, they're not."

The next morning the pigs were rolling in the mud, so Hank hosed them off, loaded them into the truck and proceeded to try again. This continued each morning for more than a week and both farmers were totally worn out.

The next morning, Hank was too tired to get out of bed, so he called to his wife, "Honey, please look outside and tell me whether them pigs are in the mud or in the grass."

She replied "neither, they're in the truck and one of them is honking the horn."

August 30th

A blonde, wanting to earn some money, decided to hire herself out as a handyman-type and started canvassing a wealthy neighbourhood. She went to the front door of the first house and asked the owner if he had any jobs for her to do.

"Well, you can paint my porch. How much will you charge?"

The blonde said, "How about 50 dollars?"

The man agreed and told her that the paint and ladders that she might need were in the garage.

The man's wife, inside the house, heard the conversation and said to her husband, "Does she realize that the porch goes all the way around the house?"

The man replied, "She should. She was standing on the porch."

A short time later, the blonde came to the door to collect her money.

"You're finished already?" he asked.

"Yes," the blonde answered, "and I had paint left over, so I gave it two coats."

Impressed, the man reached in his pocket for the $50.

"And by the way," the blonde added, "that's not a Porch, it's a Ferrari."

August 31st

Q. What is the difference between a kangaroo and a kangaroot?

A. One is an Antipodean marsupial the other is a Geordie stuck in a lift.

"You might be an autism parent when expecting the unexpected becomes the norm.'

We travel to France a lot, it is a lovely place to visit and also accessible for us. Rachel will not go in an aeroplane and until recently would suffer severe panic attacks if we even went near an airport terminal, but she will sit in the car and drive around all day, every day if we let her. Her memory is so good she can direct you from our house in England to the Eurotunnel terminal and then from Calais to Antibes, 1200 miles, to where we have a caravan. Of course we have to have break stops along the way and even though I am 'on my guard', sometimes she will do unexpected things.

Service stations on the motorways in France are huge places, some have McDonald's restaurants in them and one in the South even has a swimming pool! In the middle of summer these get packed and as with most toilet facilities there is always a queue for the women's toilets. One day I was waiting patiently with Rachel in the queue when the woman in front turned around to look for someone. Her breasts were at Rachel's eye level and she grabbed them and gave them a good squeeze. The woman looked shocked and I was horrified as I had to uncurl her fingers from them. I apologised to the woman and stood with my arms wrapped around Rachel's arms holding them tightly into her body until a cubicle came free in case she thought about squeezing or touching any other parts, and fortunately for me the woman never turned around again.

A man was also on the receiving end of Rachel's hands one day. We were pushing her through a shop in her wheelchair when a man came walking towards us, just as he reached us Rachel swung her arm out and hit him open handed and caught him in the family jewels. He bent over in agony and insisted he was 'fine' as we tried desperately hard not to laugh.

If ever the saying you need eyes in the back of your head were true it was the day Kevin went to the cricket shop. He had bought himself a new cricket bat and needed some oil and a 'knocker in-er,' – a wooden mallet to pound the bat face with. He bought them and threw the plastic bag over into the back seat of the car near Rachel. He started driving home and we heard a rustling sound behind us, before we had time to react she had the mallet out of the bag and whacked Kevin, hard, over the back of the head with it. I don't think I have ever laughed as hard in all my life but Kevin wasn't of the same opinion. We have never left a hammer near her since!

One evening we had gone down to the restaurant on the caravan site to buy a takeaway. The toilets are situated at the back of the restaurant so you have to walk past a few tables to get to them. Rachel needed the toilet and on the way to them a couple we knew were sat at a table and stopped me to say hello. Rachel reached down, picked up a lamb chop from the plate, bit it and then put it back down. I offered to buy them a new meal but they just laughed it off.

September

September 1st

An ITALIAN BOY'S CONFESSION....

'Bless me Father, for I have sinned. I have been with a loose girl'.

The priest asks, 'is that you, little Joey Pagano?'

'Yes, Father, it is.'

'And who was the girl you were with?'

'I can't tell you, Father, I don't want to ruin her reputation'

'Well, Joey, I'm sure to find out her name sooner or later so you may as well tell me now. Was it Tina Minetti?'

'I cannot say.'

'Was it Teresa Mazzarelli?'

'I'll never tell.'

'Was it Nina Capelli?'

'I'm sorry, but I cannot name her.'

Was it Cathy Piriano?'

'My lips are sealed.'

'Was it Rosa DiAngelo, then?'

'Please, Father, I cannot tell you.'

The priest sighs in frustration. 'You're very tight lipped, and I admire that. But you've sinned and have to atone. You cannot be an altar boy now for 4 months. Now you go and behave yourself.'

Joey walks back to his pew, and his friend Franco slides over and whispers, 'What'd you get?'

'Four months vacation and five good leads.'

September 2nd

Stevie Wonder and Tiger Woods in a bar.

Tiger turns to Stevie and says, 'How's the singing career going?' Stevie replies, 'Not too bad. How's the golf?'

Woods replies, 'Not too bad, I've had some problems with my swing, but I think I've got that right now.'

Stevie says, 'I always find that when my swing goes wrong, I need to stop playing for a while and not think about it. Then, the next time I play, it seems to be all right.'

Tiger says, 'You play GOLF?'

Stevie says, 'Yes, I've been playing for years'.

Tiger says, 'But -- you're blind! How can you play golf if you can't see?'

Stevie Wonder replies, 'Well, I get my caddy to stand in the middle of the fairway and call to me. I listen for the sound of his voice and play the ball towards him. Then, when I get to where the ball lands, the caddy moves to the green or farther down the fairway and again I play the ball towards his voice.'

'But, how do you putt?' asks Tiger

'Well', says Stevie, 'I get my caddy to lean down in front of the hole and call to me with his head on the ground and I just play the ball towards his voice.'

Tiger asks, 'What's your handicap?'

Stevie says, 'Well, actually -- I'm a scratch golfer.'

Woods, incredulous, says to Stevie, 'We've got to play a round sometime.'

Wonder replies, 'Well, people don't take me seriously, so I only play for money, and never play for less than $10,000 a hole. That a problem?'

Woods thinks about it and says, 'OK, I'm game for that. $10,000 a hole is fine with me. When would you like to play?'

Stevie says, 'Pick a night'

☺☺

September 3rd

A blonde woman decides that she is sick and tired of all the blonde jokes and how all blondes are perceived as stupid, so she decides to show her husband that blondes really are smart.

While her husband is out at work, she decides that she is going to paint a couple of rooms in the house.

The next day, right after her husband leaves for work, she gets down to the task at hand.

Her husband arrives home at 5:30 and smells the distinctive smell of paint. He walks into the living room and finds his wife lying on the floor in a pool of sweat.

He notices that she is wearing a ski jacket and a fur coat at the same time.

He goes over and asks her if she is OK.

She replies "yes."

He asks what she is doing.

She replies that she wanted to prove to him that not all blonde women are dumb and she wanted to do it by painting the house.

He then asks her why she has a ski jacket over her fur coat.

She replies that she was reading the directions on the paint can and they said, "For best results, put on two coats."

September 4th

Two priests were off to the showers late one night, and had undressed and stepped into the stalls before they realized there was no soap. Father John said he had some soap in his room and went to get it, not bothering to dress.

He grabbed two bars of soap, one in each hand, and headed back to the showers. He was halfway down the hall when he saw three nuns heading his way. Having no place to hide, he stood against the wall and froze like a statue.

The nuns stopped and commented on how lifelike he looked.

Then the first nun suddenly reached out and pulled on his willie.

Startled, he dropped a bar of soap.

"Oh look," said the first nun, "it's a soap dispenser."

To test her theory, the second nun also pulled on his manhood... and sure enough, he dropped the second bar of soap.

Then the third nun decided to have a go.

She pulled once, then twice, and three times - but nothing happened. Frustrated, she gave several more tugs, and then finally yelled, "Mary, Mother of God - hand lotion too!"

September 5th

After getting Pope Francis's entire luggage loaded into the limo, [and he doesn't travel light], the driver notices that the Pope is still standing by the kerbside.

"Excuse me, your Holiness." says the driver, "would you please take your seat so we can leave".

"Well to tell you the truth," says the Pope, "they never let me drive at the Vatican, and I'd really like to drive today."

"I'm sorry, but I cannot let you do that, I'd lose my job, and what if something should happen?" protests the driver, wishing he'd never gone to work that morning.

"There might be something extra in it for you." says the Pope.

Reluctantly, the driver gets in the back as the Pope climbs in behind the wheel. The driver quickly regrets his decision when, after exiting the airport, the Pontiff floors it, accelerating to 105 mph.

"Please slow down, Your Holiness!!!" pleads the worried driver, but the Pope keeps pedal to the metal until they hear sirens.

"Oh dear, I'm going to lose my licence," moans the driver. The Pope pulls over and rolls down the window as the policeman approaches, but the policeman takes one look at him, goes back to his motorcycle, and gets on the radio.

"I need to talk to the Chief," he says to the dispatcher. The Chief gets on the radio and the policeman tells him that he's stopped a limo doing a hundred and five mph. "So bust him." says the Chief.

"I don't think I can do that, he's really important," says the policeman. The Chief exclaims: "All the more reason".

"No, I mean really important", says the policeman.

The Chief than asks, "Who have you got there, the Mayor ?"

Policeman: "Bigger"

Chief: "Governor?"

Policeman: "Bigger"

"Well" says the Chief, "who is it?'

Policeman: "I think it's God"

Chief: "What makes you think it's God?"

Policeman replies: "He's got the Pope as a chauffeur!!"

☺☺

September 6th

Prince Charles goes on an unofficial visit to somewhere unpronounceable in the Australian outback.

The governor greeting him is surprised to see that despite the extreme heat and humidity the prince is wearing a fur hat with a bushy tail hanging down the back.

During the tour of the town the prince is very affable and the governor begins to feel more comfortable with him.

Eventually he picks up the courage to ask the prince "Excuse me your highness but it is very hot today. Why are you wearing that hat?"

- Well you see I told Mommy about this visit and when I told her where I was going she said "Wear the fox hat."

September 7th

On their way to get married, a young Catholic couple is involved in a fatal car accident.

The couple found themselves sitting outside the Pearly Gates waiting for St. Peter to process them into Heaven.

While waiting, they began to wonder: Could they possibly get married in Heaven? When St. Peter showed up, they asked him.

St. Peter said, "I don't know. This is the first time anyone has asked. Let me go find out,'" and he left.

The couple sat and waited, and waited.

Two months passed and the couple were still waiting.

While waiting, they began to wonder what would happen if it didn't work out; could you get a divorce in heaven.

After yet another month, St. Peter finally returned, looking somewhat bedraggled.

"Yes," he informed the couple, "You can get married in Heaven."

"Great!" said the couple, "But we were just wondering, what if things don't work out? Could we also get a divorce in Heaven?"

St. Peter, red-faced with anger, slammed his clipboard onto the ground.

"What's wrong?" asked the frightened couple.

"OH, COME ON!" St. Peter shouted, "It took me three months to find a priest up here! Do you have any idea how long it'll take me to find a lawyer?"

September 8th

Ever wondered what the difference between Grannies and Granddads is?

A 5 year old granddaughter is usually taken to school, daily, by her grandfather.

One day when he had a bad cold, Granny took the grandchild to school.

That night the little girl told her parents that the ride to school with granny was very different than with granddad!!

"What made it different?" asked her parents:

"Granny and I didn't see a single tosser, blind bastard, or frigging knobhead anywhere on the way to school."

September 9th

This young lad is out drinking, and starts chatting to a much older woman. He's only 23 years old, she's 49 and looks damn fine for her age. One thing leads to another, and the talk starts to get suggestive.

"Tell me", says the woman, "I know a lot of men fantasise about being with a mother and daughter together. I wondered if you'd be interested ....".
Well, they can't get back to her place fast enough.
She opens the front door, leads him in, and shouts up the stairs, "Mum, are you still awake?"

September 10th
Researchers for the Ministry of Transport found over 200 dead crows near greater Manchester recently, and there was concern that they may have died from Avian Flu.
A Bird Pathologist examined the remains of all the crows, and, to everyone's relief, confirmed the problem was definitely NOT Avian Flu.
The cause of death appeared to be vehicular impacts.
However, during the detailed analysis it was noted that varying colours of paints appeared on the bird's beaks and claws.
By analysing these paint residues it was determined that 98% of the crows had been killed by impact with lorries, while only 2% were killed by an impact with a car.
M of T then hired an Ornithological Behaviourist to determine if there was a cause for the disproportionate percentages of truck kills versus car kills.
The Ornithological Behaviourist very quickly concluded the cause:
--- When crows eat road kill, they always have a look-out crow in a nearby tree to warn of impending danger.
They discovered that while all the lookout crows could shout "Cah", not a single one could shout "Lorry."

☺☺

September 11th

A man walked into work on Monday with two black eyes.
His boss asked what happened.
The man said, "I was sitting behind a big woman at church.
When we stood up to sing hymns, I noticed that her dress
was caught in her crack, so I pulled it out. She turned
around and punched me square in the eye."
"Where did you get the other shiner?" the boss asked.
"Well," the man said, "I figured she didn't want it out, so I
pushed it back in."

September 12th

A guy calls a company and orders their 5-day, 10 lb. weight
loss program.
The next day, there's a knock on the door and there stands
before him a voluptuous, athletic, 19 year old babe
dressed in nothing but a pair of Nike running shoes and a
sign around her neck.
She introduces herself as a representative of the weight
loss company. The sign reads, 'If you can catch me, you
can have me.'
Without a second thought, he takes off after her. A few
miles later huffing and puffing, he finally gives up. The
same girl shows up for the next four days and the same
thing happens. On the fifth day, he weighs himself and is
delighted to find he has lost 10 lbs. as promised.
He calls the company and orders their 5-day/20 pound
program. The next day there's a knock at the door and
there stands the most stunning, beautiful, sexy woman he
has ever seen in his life. She is wearing nothing but Reebok

running shoes and a sign around her neck that reads, 'If you catch me you can have me'.

Well, he's out the door after her like a shot. This girl is in excellent shape and he does his best, but no such luck. So for the next four days, the same routine happens with him gradually getting in better and better shape.

Much to his delight on the fifth day when he weighs himself, he discovers that he has lost another 20 lbs. as promised. He decides to go for broke and calls the company to order the 7-day/50 pound program.

'Are you sure?' asks the representative on the phone. 'This is our most rigorous program.'

'Absolutely,' he replies, 'I haven't felt this good in years.'

The next day there's a knock at the door; and when he opens it he finds a huge muscular guy standing there wearing nothing but pink running shoes and a sign around his neck that reads, 'If I catch you, your backside is mine.'

He lost 63 pounds that week.'

September 13th

A married couple were on holiday in Jamaica. They were touring around the market-place looking at the goods and such, when they passed a small sandal shop.

From inside they heard the shopkeeper with a Jamaican accent say, 'You foreigners! Come in. Come into my humble shop.'

So the married couple walked in.

The Jamaican said to them, 'I 'ave some special sandals I tink you would be interested in. Dey makes you wild at sex.'

Well, the wife was really interested in buying the sandals after what the man claimed, but her husband felt he really didn't need them, being the Sex God that he was.

The husband asked the man, 'How could sandals make you a sex freak?'

The Jamaican replied, 'Just try dem on, Mon.'

Well, the husband, after some badgering from his wife, finally gave in and tried them on.

As soon as he slipped them onto his feet, he got this wild look in his eyes, something his wife hadn't seen before!!

In the blink of an eye, the husband grabbed the Jamaican, bent him over the table, yanked down his pants, ripped down his own pants, and grabbed a firm hold of the Jamaican's thighs.

The Jamaican began screaming: 'You got dem on de wrong feet!'

September 14th

An elephant was drinking out of a river one day, when he spotted a turtle asleep on a log. So, he ambled on over and kicked it clear across the river.

"What did you do that for?" asked a passing giraffe.

"Because I recognized it as the same turtle that took a nip out of my trunk 53 years ago."

"Wow, what a memory" commented the giraffe.

"Yes," said the elephant, "turtle recall".

☺☺

September 15th

An elderly couple were having dinner one evening when the husband reached across the table, took his wife's hand in his and said, "Martha, soon we will be married 50 years, and there's something I have to know. In all of these 50 years, have you ever been unfaithful to me?"

Martha replied, "Well Henry, I have to be honest with you. Yes, I've been unfaithful to you three times during these 50 years, but always for a good reason...

Henry was obviously hurt by his wife's confession, but said, "I never suspected.

Can you tell me what you mean by 'good reasons?'"

Martha said, "The first time was shortly after we were married, and we were about to lose our little house because we couldn't pay the mortgage.

Do you remember that one evening I went to see the banker and the next day he notified you that the loan would be extended?"

Henry recalled the visit to the banker and said, "I can forgive you for that. You saved our home, but what about the second time?"

Martha asked, "And do you remember when you were so sick, but we didn't have the money to pay for the heart surgery you needed? Well, I went to see your doctor one night and, if you recall, he did the surgery at no charge."

"I recall that," said Henry. "And you did it to save my life, so of course I can forgive you for that. Now tell me about the third time."

"All right," Martha said. "So do you remember when you ran for president of your golf club, and you needed 73 more votes?"

September 16th

A man and his wife walked into a dentist's office.

The man said to the dentist, "Doc, I'm in one heck of a hurry I have two buddies sitting out in my car waiting for

us to go play golf, so forget about the anaesthetic, I do not have time for the gums to get numb. I just want you to pull the tooth, and be done with it! We-have a 10:00 AM tee time at the best golf course in town and its 9:30 already ... I do not have time to wait for the anaesthetic to work!
' The dentist thought to himself, "My goodness, this is a very brave man asking to-have his tooth pulled without using anything to kill the pain."
So the dentist asks him, "Which tooth is it sir?
 "The man turned to his wife and said, "Open your mouth Honey, and show him ..."

September 17th

September 17th

In a trial, a Southern small-town prosecuting attorney called his first witness, a grandmotherly, elderly woman to the stand. He approached her and asked, 'Mrs Jones, do you know me?'
She responded, 'Why, yes, I do know you, Mr Williams. I've known you since you were a boy, and frankly, you've been a big disappointment to me. You lie, you cheat on your wife, and you manipulate people and talk about them behind their backs. You think you're a big shot when you haven't the brains to realize you'll never amount to anything more than a two-bit paper pusher. Yes, I know you.'
The lawyer was stunned. Not knowing what else to do, he pointed across the room and asked, 'Mrs Jones, do you know the defence attorney?'
She again replied, 'Why yes, I do. I've known Mr Bradley since he was a youngster, too. He's lazy, bigoted, and he has a drinking problem. He can't build a normal relationship with anyone, and his law practice is one of the

worst in the entire state. Not to mention he cheated on his wife with three different women. One of them was your wife. Yes, I know him.'

The defence attorney nearly died.

The judge asked both counsellors to approach the bench and, in a very quiet voice, said,

'If either of you idiots asks her if she knows me, I'll send you both to the electric chair.'

September 18th

A cat died and went to Heaven. God met her at the gates and said, 'You have been a good cat all these years. Anything you want is yours for the asking.'

The cat thought for a minute and then said, 'All my life I lived on a farm and slept on hard wooden floors. I would like a real fluffy pillow to sleep on.'

God said, 'Say no more.' Instantly the cat had a huge fluffy pillow.

A few days later, six mice were killed in an accident and they all went to Heaven together. God met the mice at the gates with the same offer that he made to the cat

The mice said, 'well, we have had to run all of our lives: from cats, dogs, and even people with brooms! If we could just have some little roller skates, we would not have to run again.'

God answered, 'It is done.' All the mice had beautiful little roller skates.

About a week later, God decided to check on the cat. He found her sound asleep on her fluffy pillow. God gently awakened the cat and asked, 'Is everything okay? How have you been doing? Are you happy?'

The cat replied, 'Oh, it is WONDERFUL. I have never been so happy in my life. The pillow is so fluffy, and those little Meals on Wheels you have been sending over are delicious!'

September 19th

A man is stumbling through the woods totally drunk when he comes upon a preacher baptizing people in the river. The drunk walks into the water and subsequently bumps into the preacher. The preacher turns around and is almost overcome by the smell of booze. Whereupon he asks the drunk, "Are you ready to find Jesus?"
"Yes I am" replies the drunk, so the preacher grabs him and dunks him in the river. He pulls him up and asks the drunk, "Brother have you found Jesus?"
The drunk replies, "No, I haven't."
The preacher, shocked at the answer, dunks him into the water again, but for a bit longer this time. He pulls him out of the water and asks again, "Have you found Jesus, my brother?"
The drunk again answers, "No, I have not found Jesus."
By this time the preacher is at his wits end so he dunks the drunk in the water again, but this time he holds him down for about 30 seconds.
When the drunk begins kicking his arms and legs, the preacher pulls him up. The preacher asks the drunk again, "For the love of God, have you found Jesus?"
The drunk wipes his eyes and catches his breath and says to the preacher,
"Are you sure this is where he fell in?"

September 20th

Sixty is the worst age to be," said the 60-year-old man. "You always feel like you have to pee and most of the time - you stand there and sometimes not much comes out."

"Ah, that's nothing," said the 70-year-old. "When you're seventy, you don't have a bowel movement any more. You take laxatives, eat bran, sit on the toilet all day and not much comes out!"

"Actually," said the 80-year -old, "Eighty is the worst age of all."

"Do you have trouble peeing, too?" asked the 60-year old.

"No, I pee every morning at 6:00. I pee like a racehorse on a flat track; no problem at all."

"So, do you have a problem with your bowel movement?"

"No, I have one every morning at 6:30."

Exasperated, the 60-year-old said, "You pee every morning at 6:00 and crap every morning at 6:30. So what's so bad about being 80?"

"I don't wake up until 7:00."

September 21st

The mother-in-law arrives at her daughter's house after shopping only to find her son-in-law boiling angry and hurriedly packing his suitcase.

"What happened?" she asks anxiously.

"What happened? I'll tell you what happened. I sent an e-mail to my wife telling her I was coming home today from my fishing trip. I get home... and guess what I found? Yes, your daughter, my Jean, naked with a guy in our marital bed! This is unforgivable, the end our marriage. I'm done. I'm leaving forever!"

"Calm down, calm down!" says his mother-in-law. "There is something very odd going on here. Jean would never do such a thing! There must be a simple explanation. I'll go speak to her immediately and find out what happened." Moments later, the mother-in-law comes back, a big smile on her face. "I told you there must be a simple explanation she didn't receive your email"

☺☺

September 22nd
Husband and wife are shopping at the supermarket when the man picks up a crate of Stella and sticks it into the trolley.
"What do you think you're doing?" asks the wife
"They're on offer, only £10 for 12 cans", he says
"Put them back. We can't afford it," says the wife and they carry on shopping...
A few aisles later the woman picks up a £20 jar of face cream and sticks it into the trolley.
"What do you think you're doing?" asks the man,
"It's my face cream. It makes me look beautiful," she says.
The man replies... "SO DOES 12 CANS OF STELLA AND IT'S HALF THE PRICE"

☺☺

September 23rd
A prisoner in jail received a letter from his wife:
"I have decided to plant some lettuce in the back garden. When is the best time to plant them?"
The prisoner, knowing that the prison guards read all the mail, replied in a letter:

"Dear Wife, whatever you do, DO NOT touch the back garden! That is where I hid all the gold."
A week or so later, he received another letter from his wife:
"You wouldn't believe what happened. Some men came with shovels to the house, and dug up the whole back garden."
The prisoner wrote another letter:
"Dear Wife, NOW is the best time to plant the lettuce!"

September 24th

It was entertainment night at the senior citizens' centre. After the community sing song led by Alice at the piano it was time for the Star of the Show - Claude the Hypnotist! Claude explained that he was going to put the whole audience into a trance. "Yes, each and every one of you and all at the same time." said Claude.
The excited chatter dropped to silence as Claude carefully withdrew from his waistcoat pocket a beautiful antique gold pocket watch and chain. "I want you to keep your eyes on this watch" said Claude, holding the watch high for all to see. "It is a very special and valuable watch that has been in my family for six generations" said Claude.
He began to swing the watch gently back and forth while quietly chanting "Watch the watch --- Watch the watch ---- Watch the watch"
The audience became mesmerised as the watch swayed back and forth, the lights twinkling as they were reflected from its gleaming surfaces. A hundred and fifty pairs of eyes followed the movements of the gently swaying watch.

And then, suddenly, the chain broke!!! The beautiful watch fell to the stage and burst apart on impact"
"SHIT" said Claude.
It took them three days to clean the Senior Citizens' Centre and Claude was never invited to entertain again!

September 25th
A defending attorney was cross examining a coroner. The attorney asked, "Before you signed the death certificate had you taken the man's pulse?" The coroner said, "No."
The attorney then asked, "Did you listen for a heartbeat?", and again the coroner said, "No."
Then the attorney asked, "Did you check for breathing?", and again the coroner said, "No."
"So when you signed the death certificate you had not taken any steps to make sure the man was dead, had you?"
The coroner, now tired of the brow beating said, "Well, let me put it this way. The man's brain was sitting in a jar on my desk, but for all I know he could be out there practicing law somewhere."

September 26th
A woman went into a bar in Texas County and saw a cowboy with his feet propped up on a table. He had the biggest feet she'd ever seen.
The woman asked the cowboy, if it's true what they say about men with big feet. The cowboy grinned and said, "Sure is, Maam!

Why don't you come on out to the bunk house and let me prove it to you!" The woman wanted to find out for herself, so she spent the night with him.

The next morning she handed him $200 USD. Completely surprised by the woman's action, he said, "Well, thank ya Ma'am. I'm real flattered. Ain't nobody ever paid me fer mah services before.

The woman replied, "Don't be flattered. Take the money and buy yourself a pair of decent boots that fit."

September 27th

Why don't cannibals eat clowns?

V

V

v

They taste funny.

September 28th

An elderly man, 82, just returned from the doctors only to find he didn't have long to live. So he summoned the three most important people in his life to tell them of his fate.

1. His Doctor
2. His Priest
3. His Lawyer

"Well, today I found out I don't have long to live. So I have summoned you three here, because you are the most important people in my life, and I need to ask a favour. Today, I am going to give each of you and envelope with £50,000 inside. When I die, I would ask that all three of you throw the money into my grave."

After the man passed on, the 3 people happened to run into each other. The doctor said, "I have to admit I kept £10,000 of his money, he owed me on lots of medical bills. But, I threw the other £40,000 in like he requested."
The Priest said, "I have to admit also, I kept £25,000 for the church. It's all going to a good cause. I did, however, throw the other £25,000 in the grave."
Well the Lawyer just couldn't believe what he was hearing! "I am surprised at you two taking advantage of him like that."
"I wrote a cheque for the full amount and threw it all in!"

September 29th

Two big slabs of black tarmac are in a pub resting on the bar, having a pint of beer.
When all of a sudden the pub door flies open and a big piece of red tarmac walks in.
The piece of red tarmac sits down on a stool near the bar having his pint, he starts looking around and notices the 2 black tarmacs leaning on the bar.
 The piece of red tarmac shouts at them saying "what you staring at?" and being really aggressive.
One of the pieces of black tarmac is about to reply and try to calm the piece of red tarmac down when his mate stops him and says "let's go now" and they down their drinks and promptly leave.
Once out the door the black tarmac says to his mate "why did we leave? I was only going to go and chat to him"
His pal says "no you don't do that he's a bit of a cyclepath."

September 30th

Two priests decided to go to Hawaii on vacation. They were determined to make this a real vacation by not wearing anything that would identify them as clergy.

As soon as the plane landed, they headed for a store and bought some really outrageous shorts, shirts, sandals, sunglasses, etc.

The next morning they went to the beach dressed in their "tourist" garb. They were sitting on beach chairs, enjoying a drink, the sunshine and the scenery when a "drop dead gorgeous" topless blonde in a thong bikini came walking straight towards them.

They couldn't help but stare. As the blonde passed them, she smiled and said, "Good Morning, Father, Good Morning, Father," nodding and addressing each of them individually as she passed by.

They were both stunned. How in the world did she know they were priests? So, the next day, they went back to the store and bought even more outrageous outfits. These were so loud you could hear them before you even saw them. Once again, in their new attire, the settled on the beach in their chairs to enjoy the sunshine.

After a while the same gorgeous topless blonde, wearing a string bikini bottom, and taking her sweet time, came walking toward them. Again she nodded at each of them, said "Good Morning, Father, Good Morning Father," and started to walk away. One of the Priests couldn't stand it any longer and said, "Just a minute young lady."

"Yes, Father," she said. "We are Priests and proud of it, but I have to know: How in the world did you know we are Priests, dressed as we are?

"Father, it's me -- Sister Katherine." she replied.

☺☺

"You might be an autism parent if going to the swimming pool means going ALL day!'

Rachel loves to go to the swimming pool on the caravan site but doesn't like to leave once she is in the water. We have been known to spend 6 hours a day in there. One day at Easter when the pool had just opened for the season we went in fully clothed just to test the temperature of the water. We took our shoes off and paddled in the shallow end. When we got out she went to a man who was sitting sunbathing in a chair and said 'Towel.' The man looked at me questioningly and I said 'She wants your towel.' He handed it to her and she dropped it on the ground, stamped all over it then walked off without a backward glance and left the towel on the floor.

Her pool party trick is being able to squirt water through her hands like a stream and she can direct it wherever she wants to. All the children come up and ask how she does it but it is something she has mastered by herself. When Craig was 14 or 15, he used to 'borrow her' to go and squirt girls so that he could apologise to them while pretending to pull her away and strike up a conversation with them. Little did they know that he had steered her towards them and told her to squirt them.

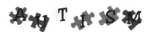

Another day Craig and his friends were pushing each other into the water, clowning around and making her laugh. When we got out of the water to go for lunch a woman was standing on the edge of the pool talking to someone. Rachel pushed her from behind, carried on walking and the woman fell into the pool. Luckily it was the shallow end, she had a bikini on and didn't make too much fuss but I ended up apologising, again.

October

October 1st
A blonde gets lost and calls for directions.
The operator asks which cross roads she's at.
The blonde replies, "I'm on the corner of Walk and Do Not Walk."

October 2nd
A redneck boy runs into his house and proclaims, "I've found the girl that I'm gonna marry! And she's a virgin!"
Incensed, his father pounds his fist on the table.
"There's no way you'll marry that girl! If she aint' good enough for her own family, she ain't good enough for ours."

October 3rd
A man visits a mate he hasn't seen for some years.
As they sit talking, a little girl walks in.
The mate introduces her as Rosedew, his daughter.
The man says "How did you get a name like that?"
His mate says "We follow the Indian practice of naming our children after the first thing we see on the day they are born. When my daughter was born I looked out of the window and saw a beautiful rose covered in dew, hence the name".
Just then, a young boy entered the room. The mate said "This is our eldest son Two dogs F***ing"

October 4th

As an airplane is about to crash, a female passenger jumps up frantically and announces, "If I'm going to die, I want to die feeling like a woman."

She removes all her clothing and asks, "Is there someone on this plane who is man enough to make me feel like a woman?"

A man stands up, removes his shirt and says, "Here, iron this!"

October 5th

I couldn't help but over-hear two guys in their mid-twenties while sitting at a bar.

One of the guys says to his buddy, "Man you look tired."

His buddy says, "Dude I'm exhausted. My girlfriend and I have sex all the time. I just don't know what to do."

A fellow about 72, sitting a couple of stools down had also over-heard the conversation. He looked over at the two young men and with the wisdom of years says, "Marry her. That'll put a stop to it!"

October 6th

A man is sitting at home alone when he hears a knock at the front door.

He opens it to find two sheriff's deputies there.

He asks if there is a problem.

One of the deputies asks if he is married.

The man replies, "Yes, I am."

The deputy then asks if he could see a picture of the man's wife.

The guy says, "Sure..." and gets a photo to show them.
The deputy says, "I'm sorry, sir. But it looks like your wife's
been hit by a truck."
The guy replies, "I know, but she has a great personality
and is an excellent cook."

October 7th

Jack wakes up with a huge hangover after the night at a
business function.
He forces himself to open his eyes and the first thing he
sees is a couple of aspirins next to a glass of water on the
side table and next to them, a single red rose!
Jack sits down and sees his clothing in front of him, all
clean and pressed.
Jack looks around the room and sees that it is in perfect
order, spotlessly clean. So is the rest of the house.
He takes the aspirins, cringes when he sees a huge black
eye staring back at him in the bathroom mirror and
notices a note on the table:
"Honey, breakfast is on the stove, I left early to go
shopping - Love you!!"
He stumbles to the kitchen and sure enough, there is hot
breakfast and the morning newspaper.
His son is also at the table, eating. Jack asks, "Son...what
happened last night?"
"Well, you came home after 3 am, drunk and out of your
mind.
You broke the coffee table, puked in the hallway and got
that black eye when you ran into the door."
"So, why is everything in such perfect order, so clean, I
have a rose and breakfast is on the table waiting for me?"

His son replies, "Oh, THAT! Mum dragged you to the bedroom and when she tried to take your pants off, you screamed, "Leave me alone, bitch, I'm married!!!"
Broken table - £585.26
Hot breakfast - £6.20
Red Rose bud - £3.00
Two aspirins – 40p
Saying the right thing, at the right time... Priceless

October 8th

The young couple invited their elderly pastor for Sunday dinner. While they were in the kitchen preparing the meal, the minister asked their son what they were having.
"Goat," the little boy replied.
"Goat?" replied the startled man of the cloth, "Are you sure about that?"
"Yep," said the youngster. "I heard Dad say to Mom, 'Today is just as good as any to have the old goat for dinner.'

October 9th

A man was on the water for his weekly fishing trip. He began his day with an 8-pound bass on the first cast and a 7-pounder on the second.
On the third cast he had just caught his first ever bass over 11 pounds when his cell phone rang.
It was a doctor notifying him that his wife had just been in a terrible accident and was in critical condition and in the ICU. The man told the doctor to inform his wife where he was and that he'd be there as soon as possible. As he hung

up he realized he was leaving what was shaping up to be his best day ever on the water.

He decided to get in a couple of more casts before heading to the hospital. He ended up fishing the rest of the morning, finishing his trip with a stringer like he'd never seen, with 3 bass over 10 pounds.

He was jubilant .

Then he remembered his wife. Feeling guilty, he dashed to the hospital. He saw the doctor in the corridor and asked about his wife's condition.

The doctor glared at him and shouted, 'You went ahead and finished your fishing trip didn't you! I hope you're proud of yourself! While you were out for the past four hours enjoying yourself on the pond, your wife has been languishing in the ICU! It's just as well you went ahead and finished, because it will be more than likely the last fishing trip you ever take!'

'For the rest of her life she will require 'round the clock care. And you'll be her care giver forever!' The man was feeling so guilty he broke down and sobbed.

The doctor then chuckled and said, 'I'm just messing with you. She's dead. What'd you catch?'

October 10th
After having dug to a depth of 10 metres in a remote area of Northern Scotland last year Scottish scientists found traces of copper wire dating back 100 years. The Scots quickly came to the conclusion that their ancestors already had a telephone network more than 100 years ago.

Not to be outdone by the Scots, English scientists dug to a depth of 20 metres somewhere in Central England. Shortly thereafter, the headlines in the English newspapers read:

"'English Archaeologists Find Traces of 200 Year Old Copper Wire!" The Brits promptly concluded that their ancestors already had an advanced high-tech communications network a hundred years earlier than the Scots.

One week later, 'The Kerryman,' an Irish newsletter, reported the following:

"After digging as deep as 30 metres in a peat bog near Tralee, Paddy O'Flanagan, a self-taught archaeologist, reported that he found absolutely nothing. Paddy has concluded that 300 years ago Ireland had already gone wireless!"

October 11th

A lonely widow, age 70, decided that it was time to get married again.

She put an ad in the local paper that read:

HUSBAND WANTED:
MUST BE IN MY AGE GROUP (70's),
MUST NOT BEAT ME,
MUST NOT RUN AROUND ON ME &
MUST STILL BE GOOD IN BED!!!!!
ALL APPLICANTS PLEASE APPLY IN PERSON .

On the second day, she heard the doorbell. Much to her dismay, she opened the door to see a grey-haired gentleman sitting in a wheelchair.

He had no arms or legs.

The old woman said, 'You're not really asking me to consider you, are you? Just look at you...you have no legs!

The old man smiled, 'Therefore, I cannot run around on you!'

She snorted. 'You don't have any arms either!'

Again, the old man smiled, 'Therefore, I can never beat you!'
She raised an eyebrow and asked intently, 'Are you still good in bed???'
The old man leaned back, beamed a big smile and said, 'Rang the doorbell didn't I?............

October 12th

Three dead bodies turn up at the mortuary, all with very big smiles on their faces. The coroner calls the police to tell them his results after the examination.
"First body: Frenchman, 60, died of heart failure whilst making love to his mistress. Hence the enormous smile, Inspector", says the Coroner.
"Second body: "Scotsman, 25, won a thousand pounds on the lottery, spent it all on whisky. Died of alcohol Poisoning, hence the smile."
The Inspector asked, "What of the third body?"
"Ah," says the coroner, "this is the most unusual one, Paddy from Dublin, 30, struck by lightning."
"Why is he smiling then?" inquires the Inspector.
"He thought he was having his picture taken."

October 13th

One morning a husband returns after several hours of fishing and decides to take a nap.
Although not familiar with the lake, the wife decides to take the boat out.
She motors out a short distance, anchors, and reads her book.

Along comes a Game Warden in his boat.
He pulls up alongside the woman and says, "Good morning, Ma'am, what are you doing?"
"Reading a book," she replies, (thinking, "Isn't that obvious?")
"You're in a Restricted Fishing Area," he informs her.
"I'm sorry, officer, but I'm not fishing, I'm reading."
"Yes, but you have all the equipment, for all I know you could start at any moment, I'll have to take you in and write you up."
"For reading a book," she replies.
"You're in a Restricted Fishing Area," he informs her again.
"I'm sorry, officer, but I'm not fishing, I'm reading."
"Yes, but you have all the equipment, for all I know you could start at any moment, I'll have to take you in and write you up."
"If you do that, I'll have to charge you with sexual assault," says the woman.
"But I haven't even touched you," says the Game Warden.
"That's true, but you have all the equipment, for all I know you could start at any moment."
"Have a nice day ma'am," and he left.
MORAL : Never argue with a woman who reads . It's likely she can also think.

October 14th
A woman meets with her lover, who is also her husband's best friend. They make love for hours.
Afterwards, as they lie in bed, the phone rings. Since it's the woman's house, she picks up the receiver. The best friend listens, only hearing her side of the conversation:

"Hello? Oh, hi... I'm so glad that you called... Really? That's wonderful... Well, I'm happy to hear you're having such a great time... Oh, that sounds terrific... Love you, too. OK. Bye-bye."

She hangs up the telephone and her lover asks, "Who was that?"

"Oh," she replies, "That was my husband telling me about the wonderful time he's having on his fishing trip with you."

October 15th

A woman was trying to board a bus, but her skirt was too tight and she couldn't step up.

She reached behind her and lowered the zipper a bit and tried again.

The skirt was still too tight. She reached behind her and lowered the zipper some more.

She still couldn't get on the bus and lowered the zipper a third time.

All of a sudden, she felt two hands on her butt, which proceeded to push her up onto the bus.

She spun around, with anger in her eyes and said very indignantly, "Sir, I do not know you well enough for you to behave in such a manner."

The man smiled coyly and said, "Lady, I don't know you well enough either for you to unzip my fly three times either!"

October 16th

Three men who were lost in the forest were captured by cannibals.

The cannibal king told the prisoners that they could live if they pass a trial.

The first step of the trial was to go to the forest and get ten pieces of the same kind of fruit. So all three men went separate ways to gather fruits.

The first one came back and said to the king, "I brought ten apples." The king then explained the trial to him. "You have to shove the fruits up your butt without any expression on your face or you'll be eaten."

The first apple went in... but on the second one he winced out in pain, so he was killed.

The second one arrived and showed the king ten berries. When the king explained the trial to him he thought to himself that this should be easy. 1...2...3...4...5...6...7...8... and on the ninth berry he burst out in laughter and was killed.

The first guy and the second guy met in heaven. The first one asked, "Why did you laugh, you almost got away with it?"

 The second one replied, "I couldn't help it, I saw the third guy coming with pineapples."

October 17th

An old man is met by his lawyer, and is told he is going to be audited. He rides to the Inland Revenue office with his lawyer, and when he gets there, he begins to talk with the tax officer.

"I bet £2,000 I can bite my own eye!" The tax officer agrees to the bet, believing it an impossible task.

The old man laughs, pulls out his glass eye, and bites it. The tax officer is dumbfounded.

The old man bets £3,000 he can bite his other eye. The tax officer knows there's no way possible to do this, so he once more agrees.

The old man cackles, pulls out his dentures, and bites his eye.

Then the old man finally wagers, "I bet £20,000 I can stand on the far side of your desk, pee over the desk, and get it into your wastebasket, without missing a single drop."

The tax officer knows he won't be able to, so once more he agrees. The old man indeed misses, peeing all over the desk, and on the paperwork.

The tax officer jumps for joy, but then notices the lawyer over in the corner moaning.

"Are you all right?" asks the agent.

"No! On the way over here, he bet me £400,000 he could pee on your desk and you'd be happy about it!"

October 18th

An Irish priest and a Rabbi found themselves sharing a compartment on a train.

After a while, the priest opened a conversation by saying "I know that, in your religion, you're not supposed to eat pork...Have you actually ever tasted it?

The Rabbi said, "I must tell the truth. Yes, I have, on the odd occasion."

Then the Rabbi had his turn of interrogation. He asked, "Your religion, too... I know you're supposed to be celibate. But...."

The priest replied, "Yes, I know what you're going to ask. I have succumbed once or twice."

There was silence for a while. Then the Rabbi peeped around the newspaper he was reading and said, "Better than pork, isn't it?"

October 19th
A Captain in the foreign legion was transferred to a desert outpost. On his orientation tour he noticed a very old, seedy looking camel tied out back of the enlisted men's barracks. He asked the Sergeant leading the tour, "What's the camel for?"
The Sergeant replied "Well sir it's a long way from anywhere, and the men have natural sexual urges, so when they do, uh, we have the camel."
The captain said "Well if it's good for moral, then I guess it's all right with me."
After he had been at the fort for about 6 months the captain could not stand it anymore so he told his Sergeant, "BRING IN THE CAMEL!!!"
The sarge shrugged his shoulders and led the camel into the captain's quarters. The captain got a foot stool & proceeded to have vigorous sex with the camel.
As he stepped, satisfied, down from the stool, and was buttoning his pants he asked the Sergeant, "Is that how the enlisted men do it?"
The Sergeant replied, "Well sir, they usually just use it to ride into town."

October 20th
A blonde woman gets a job as a physical education teacher of 16 year olds.

She notices a boy at the end of the field standing alone, while all the other kids are running around having fun, kicking a football.

She takes pity on him and decides to speak to him.

You ok? She asks.

Yes, he replies.

You can go and play with the other kids, you know, she says.

It's best if I stay here, he says.

Whys that, sweetie? asks the blonde.

The boy looks at her incredulously and says: "because I'm the goal keeper!!!"

October 21st

A priest is walking down the street and a women standing on the corner calls to him and says "Hey father, you want a quickie, only £5". The priest promptly says "No Thanks" and continues down the street.

A little while later another women calls from a door way of a building and says "Hey father, you want a quickie, only £5". The priest again says "No Thanks" and continues down the street.

Another while later another women calls from a window of a building and yells down "Hey father, you want a quickie, only £5". The priest again says "No Thanks" and continues down the street.

He finally gets back to his parish and goes up to one of the sisters there. He asks her "What's a Quickie?" to which she promptly replies "£5, the same as in town."

October 22ⁿᵈ

I got banned from Waterstones today for moving all the 'Caution - Wet Floor' signs to the '50 Shades of Grey' shelf.

October 23ʳᵈ

Two married buddies are out drinking one night when one turns to the other and says, "You know, I don't know what else to do. Whenever I go home after we've been out drinking, I turn the headlights off before I get to the driveway. I shut off the engine and sneak up the stairs, I get undressed in the bathroom. I ease into bed and my wife STILL wakes up and yells at me for staying out so late!"

His buddy looks at him and says, "Well, you're obviously taking the wrong approach. I screech into the driveway, slam the door, storm up the steps, throw my shoes into the closet, jump into bed, slap her on the butt and say, "You as horny as I am? And she always acts like she's sound asleep!"

October 24ᵗʰ

Far away in the tropical waters of the Caribbean, two prawns were swimming around in the sea, one called Justin and the other called Christian. The prawns were constantly being harassed and threatened by sharks that inhabited the area.

Finally one day Justin said to Christian, "I'm fed up with being a prawn I wish I was a shark, and then I wouldn't have any worries about being eaten."

A large mysterious cod appeared and said, "Your wish is granted."

Lo and behold, Justin turned into a shark.

Horrified, Christian immediately swam away, afraid of being eaten by his old mate.

Time passed (as it invariably does) and Justin found life as a shark boring and lonely. All his old mates simply swam away whenever he came close to them. Justin didn't realize that his new menacing appearance was the cause of his sad plight.

While swimming alone one day he saw the mysterious cod again and he thought perhaps the mysterious fish could change him back into a prawn. He approached the cod and begged to be changed back, and, lo and behold, he found himself turned back into a prawn.

With tears of joy in his tiny little eyes Justin swam back to his friends and bought them all a cocktail . Looking around the gathering at the reef he realized he couldn't see his old pal.

"Where's Christian?" he asked.

"He's at home, still distraught that his best friend changed sides to the enemy and became a shark," came the reply.

Eager to put things right again and end the mutual pain and torture, He set off to Christian's abode. As he opened the coral gate, memories came flooding back. He banged on the door and shouted: "It's me, Justin, your old friend, come out and see me again."

Christian replied, "No way man, you'll eat me. You're now a shark, the enemy, and I'll not be tricked into being your dinner."

Justin cried back "No, I'm not. That was the old me. I've changed........."

"I've found Cod. I'm a Prawn again Christian."

☺☺

October 25th

It was a hot Saturday evening in the summer of 1960 and
Fred had a date with Peggy Sue. He arrived at her house
and rang the bell.

'Oh, come on in!' Peggy Sue's mother said as she
welcomed Fred in. 'Have a seat in the living room. Would
you like something to drink? Lemonade? Iced tea?'

'Iced tea, please,' Fred said. Mum brought the iced tea.

'So, what are you and Peggy planning to do tonight?' she
asked.

'Oh, probably catch a movie, then maybe grab a bite to eat
at the local cafe, maybe take a walk on the beach...'

'Peggy likes to screw, you know,' Mum informed him.

'Really?' Fred asked, eyebrows rose.

'Oh yes,' the mother continued. 'When she goes out with
her friends, that's all they do!'

'Is that so?' asked Fred, incredulous.

'Yes,' said the mother. 'As a matter of fact, she'd screw all
night if we let her!'

'Well, thanks for the tip!' Fred said as he began thinking
about alternate plans for the evening.

A moment later, Peggy Sue came down the stairs looking
pretty as a picture wearing a pink blouse and a hoop skirt,
and with her hair tied back in a bouncy ponytail. She
greeted Fred.

'Have fun, kids!' the mother said as they left.

Half an hour later, a completely dishevelled Peggy Sue
burst into the house and slammed the front door behind
her.

'Twist, Mum!' she angrily yelled to her mother in the
kitchen. 'The Twist, Dammit! It's called the Twist!'

☺☺

October 26th

A soldier ran up to a nun.
Out of breath he asked, "Please, Sister, may I hide under your skirt. I'll explain later."
The nun agreed.
A moment later two Military Police ran up and asked, "Sister, have you seen a soldier?"
The nun replied, "He went that way."
After the MP's ran off, the soldier crawled out from under her skirt and said,
"I can't thank you enough, Sister. You see, I don't want to go to Iraq."
The nun said, "I understand completely."
The soldier added, "I hope I'm not being rude, but you have a great pair of legs!"
The nun replied, "If you had looked a little higher, you would have seen a great pair of balls. I don't want to go to Iraq, either."

October 27th

John had been courting Sarah for some time and finally decided that he wished to spend the rest of his life with her. So, he duly proposed, Sarah accepted, and the wedding preparations began.
The only aspect of his relationship that disturbed John was to do with Sarah's younger sister, Amy. Ever since the engagement had been announced, Amy had been flirting with John. Small glances when he had dinner with the family, a seductive glance here, even the occasional wink there. Since Amy was a very attractive young lady, and

since John did not want to upset his bride-to-be, he decided to keep this to himself, thinking it would pass with time and would not have to be mentioned again.

John was wrong. As the date of the wedding drew closer, the flirtation from Amy grew. She began finding excuses for small bodily contacts, being more open with her glances and her suggestive behaviour. Three days before the wedding, John received a text from Amy saying:

"John, please come round to my house to help with some heavy lifting. Don't mention to Sarah xxx"

Knowing that he couldn't ignore his soon-to-be sister-in-law, John steeled himself and went round to Amy's house as requested. There was a note on the front door telling him to let himself in. As he entered the hallway, he saw Amy at the top of her stairs - near naked! She winked at John, beckoned with her finger and walked seductively off in the direction of her bedroom.

John immediately turned straight round and marched out of the house. No sooner had he set foot outside than his prospective father-in-law appeared, saying:

"John, I am so proud of you. Amy has been doing all of this to test your devotion to my Sarah, and I have to say that you have proved yourself a worthy son-in-law. I am proud to welcome you to my family!"

The motto of the story:

Always, always, always... leave your condoms in the car.

October 28th

Fresh from her shower, a woman stood in front of the mirror complaining to her husband that her breasts were too small.

Instead of romantically telling her this is not true, he uncharacteristically comes up with a suggestion: "If you want your breasts to grow, then take a piece of toilet paper and rub it between them for a few seconds every day"

Willing to try anything, she got a piece of toilet paper and stood in front of the mirror, rubbing it between her breasts.

How long will this take?" she asked.

They will grow larger over a period of years," her husband replied.

She stopped rubbing and said. "Do you really think rubbing a piece of toilet paper between my breasts every day will make my breasts larger over the years?"

Without missing a beat he said "Worked for your arse, didn't it?"

October 29th

Little Tony was 9 years old and was staying with his grandmother for a few days.

He'd been playing outside with the other kids for a while when he came into the house and asked her,

'Grandma, what's that called when two people sleep in the same room and one is on top of the other?'

She was a little taken aback, but she decided to tell him the truth.

'It's called sexual intercourse, darling.'

Little Tony said, 'Oh, OK,' and went back outside to play with the other kids.

A few minutes later he came back in and said angrily, 'Grandma, it isn't called sexual intercourse.

It's called Bunk Beds.............. And Jimmy's mum wants to talk to you.'

☺☺

October 30th
A man is in bed with his Thai girlfriend.
After having great sex, she spends the next hour just stroking his manhood, something she had lovingly done on many occasions.
Rather enjoying it, he turns and asks her, "Why do you love doing that?"
She replies: "Because I really miss mine".

☺☺

October 31st
I saw a homeless man sleeping inside a big cardboard box outside the train station this morning.
Not wanting to disturb him, I crept over and put a Starbucks coffee cup on top of his box.
He immediately woke up and said, "Thank you."
"No problem." I smiled.
He looked at me again and said, "It's empty."
I said, "I know, it's meant to be a chimney."

☺☺

'You might be an autism parent if here are lines and lines and LINES of small toys all over the place'

Or in our case, cassette tapes!

Rachel has over 500 cassettes and has used and broken probably more than 100 Walkman's and even more headphones. She has always been sensitive to loud noises. If the grounds man came to school to mow the grass they would have to shut all the windows in the classroom. She couldn't stay in cookery lessons if they were using a mixer or in the design technology class if they were using a drill. When having renovations done at home the builders would have to leave when she returned home from school and if they had a small job to finish I would have to take her for a walk until they were finished.

Music is an absolute godsend to us. We use music to drown out noises she doesn't like – lawnmowers, drills, sirens, babies crying, motorbikes, trucks etc. At school she started to wear headphones and carry a cassette Walkman around with her. Nowadays they go everywhere with her and we always have several spares in reserve in case they break.

One day we went to a well-known electrical store to replace a broken Walkman and took out the product replacement insurance for £2.99 so that it could be exchanged for a new one if it got broken. We smiled knowingly at each other on our way out of the shop because we knew we had a good deal. It was a sad day when, eighteen Walkman's later and on first name terms with the staff in the shop, they stopped stocking them and refunded our £2.99.

If a tape gets broken we have to physically show it to her going into the bin and she will never ever ask or look for it again. Likewise if one gets mislaid, under a book or settee for example she will wander around looking high and low saying where, where, where and find it, find it, until it is found. We are fortunate enough to have very good friends who scour charity shops and car boot sales and pick up any new tapes or Walkman's that they see. Every day she will sit and record herself singing, other people singing and reading stories, parts of DVD's that she likes and things she finds on YouTube. Besides taping her music and DVD's she also tapes conversations that are going on in the background and one of these days she will play the tape back and get someone in trouble.

One day we had friends over and she was playing a tape pretty loud. She likes to watch people doing exercises and had stumbled across Linda Hamilton in the Terminator doing pull-ups. If you haven't seen it I suggest you google it with the sound on. As she does every pull-up she makes a grunting noise, which, without the film to watch could pass as love making sounds. Of course myself and Kevin knew what it was and burst out laughing when our friends started eyeing each other suspiciously and looking embarrassed.

 She colour codes all the tapes and the cardboard inserts and draws and makes her own inserts from paper. She is the only one who knows the system and she makes trains all across the floor. Sometimes they are seven metres long and three or four tapes deep. We have to walk through the lounge room like ninjas, being very careful not to stand on them or nudge them out of line with our feet because it is a national disaster if we do!

November

November 1st

Two engineering students were walking across campus when one said, "Where did you get such a great bike?" The second engineer replied, "Well, I was walking along yesterday minding my own business when a beautiful woman rode up on this bike. She threw the bike to the ground, took off all her clothes and said, 'Take what you want.'"

The second engineer nodded approvingly, "Good choice; the clothes probably wouldn't have fit."

November 2nd

While walking through Golden Gate Park in San Francisco, a man came upon another man hugging a tree with his ear firmly against the tree. Seeing this he inquired, 'Just out of curiosity, what the heck are you doing?'

'I'm listening to the music of the tree,' the other man replied.

'You've gotta be kiddin' me.'

'No, would you like to give it a try?'

Understandably curious, the man says, 'Well, OK...' So he wrapped his arms around the tree and pressed his ear up against it. With this, the other guy slapped a pair of handcuffs on him, took his wallet, jewellery, car keys, then stripped him naked and left.

Two hours later another nature lover strolled by, saw this guy handcuffed to the tree stark naked, and asked, 'What the heck happened to you?'

He told the guy the whole terrible story about how he got there.

When he finished telling his story, the other guy shook his head in sympathy, walked around behind him, kissed him gently behind the ear and said, 'This just isn't gonna be your day, cupcake...'

November 3rd

The Italian Secret to a Long Marriage
At St. Peter's Catholic Church in Adelaide, they have weekly husbands' marriage seminars.
At the session last week, the priest asked Giuseppe, who said he was approaching his 50th wedding anniversary, to take a few minutes and share some insight into how he had managed to stay married to the same woman all these years.
Giuseppe replied to the assembled husbands, 'Wella, I'va tried to treat her nicea, spenda da money on her, but besta of all is, I tooka her to Italy for the 25th anniversary!'
The priest responded, 'Giuseppe, you are an amazing inspiration to all the husbands here! Please tell us what you are planning for your wife for your 50th anniversary?'

Giuseppe proudly replied, " I gonna go pick her up."

November 4th

After two weeks on a desert island with only each other for company, Bob and Geoff are getting horny.
"Look," says Bob, "Neither of us are gay, but if you pretend to be a women for me, when I'm done, I'll pretend to be a woman for you."
Geoff reluctantly agrees and suffers 10 minutes of painful humiliation as Bob takes him from behind.
When it's over, Geoff asks Bob for his go.

"No," Bob replies, "I've got a headache."

November 5th
Paddy phones an ambulance because his mate's been hit by a car.
Paddy: 'Get an ambulance here quick, he's bleeding from his nose and ears and I think both his legs are broken.'
Operator: 'What is your location sir?'
Paddy: 'Outside number 28 Eucalyptus Street.'
Operator: 'How do you spell that sir?'
Silence.... heavy breathing.
And after a minute.
Operator: 'Are you there sir?'
Silence …… and more heavy breathing.
 And another minute later.'
Operator: 'Sir, can you hear me?'
This goes on for another few minutes until....'
Operator: 'Sir, please answer me. Can you still hear me?'
Paddy: 'Yes, sorry `bout dat... I couldn't spell eucalyptus, so I just dragged him round to number 3 Oak Street.

November 6th
With all the new technology regarding fertility recently, a 75-year-old friend of mine was able to give birth.
When she was discharged from the hospital and went home, I went to visit.
'May I see the new baby?' I asked
'Not yet,' she said 'I'll make coffee and we can chat for a while first.'
Thirty minutes had passed, and I asked, 'May I see the new baby now?'

'No, not yet,' She said.
After another few minutes had elapsed,
I asked again, 'May I see the baby now?'
'No, not yet,' replied my friend.
Growing very impatient, I asked, 'Well, when can I see the baby?'
'WHEN HE CRIES!' she told me.
'WHEN HE CRIES?' I demanded. 'Why do I have to wait until he CRIES?'
'BECAUSE I FORGOT WHERE I PUT HIM, O.K.?!!'

November 7th
Paddy says to Mick "I found this pen, is it yours?"
Mick replies "Don't know, give it here."
He then tries it and says, "Yes it is"
Paddy asks "How do you know?"
Mick replies, "That's my handwriting."

November 8th
A pharmacist returns from his lunch break to find a man leaning against the counter in a very tense way.
"What's the matter with him?" he asks his new, pretty blonde assistant.
"He came in with a really bad cough, and asked me for some strong cough medicine", she replied. "I couldn't find any on the shelf, so I gave him a strong laxative instead. He swallowed the lot!"
"You stupid girl", the pharmacist yelled. "Laxatives won't cure a cough"

"They're working for him" she pointed out. He's been standing there for ages, without moving, and he hasn't coughed once since he took them!"

November 9th
A seriously depressed woman stands at the edge of a cliff, trying to get the nerve up to jump.
A passing tramp stops and says, "Since you're about to kill yourself anyway, would you mind if we had sex first?"
The woman said "Hell no ... you pervert .... get away from me!"
The tramp turned to leave and muttered, "Fine, I'll just go wait at the bottom."

November 10th
A doctor tells an old couple at his office he needs to get a stool sample, a urine sample, and a blood test from the old man.
Hard of hearing, the old man asks his wife what the doctor said.
The wife replies, "He needs a pair of your underwear."

November 11th
Old Mabel lives in the nursing home. She's a bit senile and a right character, and loves whizzing around at high speed in her wheelchair. The staff and other residents have a habit of playing good-natured pranks on her.

One day she's hurtling along the corridor when another resident stands in front of her, holds his hand up and tells her to stop. "Can I see your driving licence please madam", he says. She rummages about in her handbag, pulls out an old bus ticket and shows it to the man. "Very good, madam, you may go on your way".

So off she goes, to be confronted a little later on by another old man. "Can I see your insurance documents, please madam". She has another rummage in her handbag, pulls out an old sweet wrapper, and shows it to him. "Thank you madam, that's all in order, off you go". Round the next corner she comes across a male nurse standing there with his trousers around his ankles.

"Oh no", she says, "Not the breathalyser again!"

November 12th

A man sunbathes in the nude and ends up burning his penis.

His doctor tells him to ease the pain by dipping it in a cup of cold milk.

Later, his blonde girlfriend comes home and finds him with his penis in a cup of cold milk.

'Good heavens', she remarks, 'I always wondered how you guys re-loaded those things!'

November 13th

On a sticky hot summers day, a man got out of the shower and said to his wife, "Honey, it's just too hot to wear any clothes today. What do you think the neighbours would say if I mowed the lawn with nothing on?"

His wife smiled sweetly, and replied, "I think they'd say I married you for your money."

November 14th
Dorothy and Edna, two widows, are talking.

Dorothy: "That nice George Johnson asked me out for a date. I know you went out with him last week, and I wanted to talk with you about him before I give him my answer."

Edna: "Well, I'll tell you. He shows up at my apartment punctually at 7pm, dressed like such a gentleman in a fine suit, and he brings me such beautiful flowers! Then he takes me downstairs. And what's there: a limousine, uniformed chauffeur and all. Then he takes me out for dinner; a marvellous dinner, lobster, champagne, dessert, and after-dinner drinks. Then we go see a show. Let me tell you Dorothy, I enjoyed it so much I could have just died from pleasure! So then we are coming back to my apartment and he turns into an ANIMAL. Completely crazy, he tears off my expensive new dress and has his way with me three times!!!"

Dorothy: "Goodness gracious!... so you are telling me I shouldn't go ??".

Edna: "No, no, no... course not... I'm just saying, wear an old dress".

November 15th
Teacher asks the kids in class: "What do you want to be when you grow up?

Little Johnny: "I wanna be a billionaire, going to the most expensive clubs, take the best bitch with me, give her a Ferrari worth over a million quid, an apartment in Copacabana, a mansion in Paris , a jet to travel through Europe , an Infinite Visa Card and to make love to her three times a day".

The teacher, shocked, and not knowing what to do with the bad behaviour of the child decides not to give importance to what he said and then continues the lesson. And you, Susie?

"I wanna be Johnny's bitch."

November 16th

A tired looking man was eating in a truck stop when three Hell's Angels bikers strolled in.

Looking for trouble, the first biker walked up, pushed his cigarette into the man's pie, and then took a seat at the counter.

The second Hell's Angel walked up to the man, spat into his coffee, and also took a seat at the counter.

The third walked up to the man, turned over his plate, and took a seat at the counter.

Without a word of protest, the man got up and quietly left the diner.

 One of the bikers said to the waitress, "Well, he isn't much of a man is he? He didn't even defend himself!"

The waitress smiled and replied, "He's not much of a truck driver, either. He just backed his big rig over three shiny motorbikes."

November 17th

Paddy's wife comes home from work to find he has nailed all her sex toys to the wall...

She shouts "You stupid useless sod, I said I wanted a 'dado' rail...

November 18th

The old man placed an order for one hamburger, French fries and a drink.

He unwrapped the plain hamburger and carefully cut it in half, placing one half in front of his wife.

He then carefully counted out the French fries, dividing them into two piles and neatly placed one pile in front of his wife.

He took a sip of the drink; his wife took a sip and then set the cup down between them. As he began to eat his few bites of hamburger, the people around them were looking over and whispering.

Obviously they were thinking, ' That poor old couple - all they can afford is one meal for the two of them. '

As the man began to eat his fries a young man came to the table and politely offered to buy another meal for the old couple. The old man said, they were just fine - they were used to sharing everything

People closer to the table noticed the little old lady hadn't eaten a bite. She sat there watching her husband eat and occasionally taking turns sipping the drink.

Again, the young man came over and begged them to let him buy another meal for them.

This time the old woman said ' No, thank you, we are used to sharing everything. '

Finally, as the old man finished and was wiping his face neatly with the napkin, the young man again came over to the little old lady who had yet to eat a single bite of food and asked ' What is it you are waiting for? '

She answered -- 'THE TEETH'.

☺☺

November 19th

An 80 year old woman was arrested for shop lifting.
 When she went before the Judge he asked her, "What did you steal?"

She replied:" a can of peaches".

The Judge asked her why she had stolen them and she replied that she was hungry.

The Judge then asked her how many peaches were in the can. She replied "six".

The Judge then said, "Well, I will consider giving you six days in jail." Before the Judge could actually pronounce the sentence the woman's husband spoke up and asked the Judge if he could address the court.

The Judge agreed, thinking that he was going to ask him to be lenient on his wife, considering her age.

The husband then said, "I want to inform your honour, that she also stole a can of peas."

☺☺

November 20th

On a beautiful summer's day, two American tourists were driving through Wales .

At
Llanfairpwllgwyngyllgogerychwyrndrobwyllllantysiliogogoc

h, they stopped for lunch, and one of the tourists asked the waitress,
'Before we order, I wonder if you could settle an argument for us.
Can you pronounce where we are, very, very, very slowly?'..........
The girl leaned over and said,
'Burrr ... gurrr ... king'

November 21st
A dog lover, whose dog was a female and "in heat', agreed to look after her neighbours' male dog while the neighbours' were on vacation.
She had a large house and believed that she could keep the two dogs apart. However, as she was drifting off to sleep she heard awful howling and moaning sounds, rushed downstairs and found the dogs locked together, in obvious pain and unable to disengage, as so frequently happens when dogs mate.
Unable to separate them, and perplexed as to what to do next, although it was late, she called the vet, who answered in a very grumpy voice.
Having explained the problem to him, the vet said,
"Hang up the phone and place it down alongside the dogs. I will then call you back and the noise of the ringing will make the male lose his erection and he will be able to withdraw."
"Do you think that will work?" she asked.
"Just worked on me," he replied....

☺☺

November 22nd

An Italian husband and his wife were having a meal at a very fine restaurant when this absolutely stunning young woman comes over to their table, gives the husband a big open mouthed kiss, then says she'll meet him later and walks away.

The wife looks at her husband and says, "Who was that?"

"Oh," says the husband, "She's my mistress"

"Well that's the last straw," says the wife. "I've had enough, I want a divorce!"

"I can understand that," replies the husband, "but remember, if we get a divorce it will mean no more shopping trips to Paris, no more wintering in Barbados, no more summers in Tuscany, no more Jaguar in the garage and no more yacht club. No more credit card and large bank accounts. But the decision is yours."

Just then, a mutual friend enters the restaurant with a gorgeous babe on his arm.

"Who's that woman with Tony?" asks the wife.

"That's his mistress," says the husband.

"Ours is prettier," she replies.

November 23rd

An Englishman's wife steps up to the tee and, as she bends over to place her ball, a gust of wind blows her skirt up and reveals her lack of underwear.

'Good God, Daphne! Why aren't you wearing any knickers?' he demands...

'Well you don't give me enough housekeeping money to afford any.'

He immediately reaches into his pocket and says, 'For the sake of decency, here's £50. Go and buy yourself some underwear.'

Next, the Irishman's wife bends over to set her ball on the tee ...her skirt also flies up to show that she is not wearing any knickers either.

'Sweet mudder of Jaysus! Bridget! Where are your knickers?'

She replies, 'I can't afford any on the allowance you give me.' He reaches into his pocket and says, 'For the sake of decency, here's £20. Go and buy yourself some underwear!'

Lastly, the Scotsman's wife bends over. The wind also takes her skirt over her head to reveal that she too is naked under it.

'Jesus, Mary and Joseph, Aggie. Where the frig are yer drawers?'

She also explains, 'You dinna give me enough money ta be able taaffarrd any.'

He reaches into his pocket and says, 'Well, fer the love o' Jaysus 'n the sake of decency...here's a comb. Tidy yerself up a wee bit.'

November 24th

A Doctor was addressing a large audience in Tampa. 'The material we put into our stomach is enough to have killed most of us sitting here, years ago. Red meat is awful. Soft drinks corrode your stomach lining. Chinese food is loaded with MSG. High fat diets can be disastrous, and none of us realizes the long-term harm caused by the germs in our drinking water. However, there is one thing that is the most dangerous of all and we all have eaten, or will eat it.

Can anyone here tell me what food it is that causes the most grief and suffering for years after eating it?'
After several seconds of quiet, a 75-year-old man in the front row raised his hand, and softly said, 'Wedding Cake.'

November 25th
A newlywed couple arrived back from honeymoon to move into their tiny new flat.
"Care to go to bed?" the husband asked.
"Shh!" said his blushing bride. "These walls are paper thin. The neighbours will know what you mean! Next time, ask me in code - like, 'Have you left the washing machine door open' - instead."
So, the following night, the husband asks: "I don't suppose you left the washing machine door open, darling?"
"No," she snapped back, "I definitely shut it." Then she rolled over and fell asleep.
The next morning, she woke up feeling a little frisky herself, so she nudged her husband and said: "I think I did leave the washing machine door open after all..."
"Don't worry," said the man. "It was only a small load so I did it by hand."

November 26th
A drunken man is walking along the street at 1.00am. A policeman stops him and asks "Where are you going?"
The man replies "I'm going to a lecture on alcohol abuse and the dangers it causes to one's physical health and mental well-being."

The policeman enquires, "Who gives lectures on that at this time of night?"
The man replies "My Wife!"

November 27th

A paramedic is called to a woman in labour at home.
Only a 4yr old girl is there with mum so he asks her to hold mum's hand while he is delivering the baby.
When it's all over he asks the little girl what she thinks about her new brother.
She say's "Slap the little bugger again; he should never have crawled in there."

November 28th

The husband leans over and asks his wife, 'Do you remember the first time we had sex together over fifty years ago?
We went behind the village tavern where you leaned against the back fence and I made love to you.'
'Yes', she says, 'I remember it well.'
'OK,' he says, 'How about taking a stroll around there again and we can do it for old time's sake?'
'Oh Jim, you old devil, that sounds like a crazy, but good idea!'
A police officer sitting in the next booth heard their conversation and, having a chuckle to himself, he thinks to himself, I've got to see these two old-timers having sex against a fence. I'll just keep an eye on them so there's no trouble.
So he follows them.

The elderly couple walks haltingly along, leaning on each other for support aided by walking sticks..

Finally, they get to the back of the tavern and make their way to the fence.

The old lady lifts her skirt and the old man drops his trousers.

As she leans against the fence, the old man moves in.

Then suddenly they erupt into the most furious sex that the policeman has ever seen.

This goes on for about ten minutes while both are making loud noises and moaning and screaming.

Finally, they both collapse, panting on the ground.

The policeman is amazed.

He thinks he has learned something about life and old age that he didn't know.

After about half an hour of lying on the ground recovering, the old couple struggles to their feet and puts their clothes back on.

The policeman is still watching and thinks to himself, this is truly amazing; I've got to ask them what their secret is.

So, as the couple passes, he says to them, 'Excuse me, but that was something else. You must've had a fantastic sex life together. Is there some sort of secret to this?'

Shaking, the old man is barely able to reply,

'Fifty years ago that wasn't an electric fence!

November 29th

A passenger in a taxi leaned over to ask the driver a question and gently tapped him on the shoulder to get his attention.

The driver screamed, lost control of the cab, nearly hit a bus, drove up over the curb and stopped just inches from a large plate glass window.

For a few moments everything was silent in the cab.

Then, the still shaking Driver said, 'Are you OK? I'm so sorry, but you scared the daylights out of me.'

The badly shaken passenger apologized to the driver and said he didn't realize that a mere tap on the shoulder would startle the driver so badly.

The driver replied, 'No, no, I'm the one who is sorry, it's entirely my Fault. Today is my very first day driving a cab . . . . I've been driving a hearse for the past 25 years.

November 30th

In a small town, an elderly couple had been dating each other for a long time.

At the urging of their friends, they decided it was finally time for marriage.

Before the wedding, they went out to dinner and had a long conversation regarding how their marriage might work.

They discussed finances, living arrangements and so on.

Finally, the old gentleman decided it was time to broach the subject of their physical relationship.

"How do you feel about sex?" he asked, rather trustingly.

"Well," she said, responding very carefully, "I'd have to say... I would like it infrequently."

The old gentleman sat quietly for a moment, and then over his glasses, he looked her in the eye and casually asked............

"Is that one word or two?"

'You might be an autism parent if you've learned a whole new language, and you're used to strangers looking to you for translation because they couldn't understand a word your child said'

Definitely! Rachel has her own words for different things. At night time she says 'slippers next morning' translated that means 'if I put my slippers on we can stay in all day and not go out.' She says 'goodbye hoskital' a lot which means 'we are not going to the hospital.' Shops are known by the colour of their advertising signs – blue shop, green shop, red shop, a DIY shop is the 'drill shop' and the pet shop is 'animals'.   A few other words that she has made up are :-

Loomy = Naomi

Black = MP3 player

Cartrain = Eurotunnel

Watching = DVD player

Listening = headphones

Colours = pens

Swish = windscreen wipers

Pram = wheelchair

Whitehouse = our caravan

Lissy = Tissue

Johnsons = Doctor (our family doctor was Dr Johnson)

White = drawing paper

December

December 1st
An elderly couple are at home watching the TV. The husband has the remote and is constantly switching between a programme on fishing and the porn channel. His wife is getting more and more agitated and finally says, For goodness sake, leave it on the porn channel ...You know how to fish.

December 2nd
A guy sitting at a bar at Heathrow Terminal 3 noticed a really beautiful woman sitting next to him.
He thought to himself: "Wow, she's so gorgeous she must be an off duty flight attendant. But which airline does she work for?"
Hoping to pick her up, he leaned towards her and uttered the Delta slogan: "Love to fly and it shows?"
She gave him a blank, confused stare and he immediately thought to himself: "Damn, she doesn't work for Delta."
A moment later, another slogan popped into his head. He leaned towards her again, "Something special in the air?"
She gave him the same confused look. He mentally kicked himself, and scratched Singapore Airlines off the list.
Next he tried the Thai Airways slogan: "Smooth as Silk."
This time the woman turned on him, "What the Friigggggging hell do you want?"
The man smiled, then slumped back in his chair, and said "Ahhhhh, Ryanair!!

December 3rd

Two women friends had gone out for a girl's night out, and had been overenthusiastic on the cocktails.

Incredibly drunk and walking home, they suddenly realized they both needed to pee.

They were very close to a graveyard, and one of them suggested they do their business behind a headstone or something.

The first woman had nothing to wipe with, so she took off her panties, used them, and threw them away.

Her friend however, was wearing an expensive underwear set and didn't want to ruin hers, but was lucky enough to salvage a large ribbon from a wreath that was on a grave and proceeded to wipe herself with it.

After finishing, they made their way home.

The next day, the first woman's husband phones the other husband and says, "These girls' nights out have got to stop. My wife came home last night without her panties."

"That's nothing," said the other. "Mine came back with a sympathy card stuck between the cheeks of her butt that said, "From all of us at the fire station, we'll never forget you!"

December 4th

One night a man walks into a bar looking sad. The bartender asks the man what he wants.

The man says "Oh just a beer".

The bartender asked the man "What's wrong, why are you so down today?"

The man said "My wife and I got into a fight, and she said she wouldn't talk to me for a month".

The bartender said "So what's wrong with that"?

The man said "Well the month is up tonight".

December 5th

A young Chinese couple gets married. She's a virgin. Truth be told, he is a virgin too, but she doesn't know that.
 On their wedding night, she cowers naked under the sheets as her husband undresses in the darkness.
He climbs into bed next to her and tries to be reassuring.
"My darring," he whispers, "I know dis your firss time and you berry
Frighten. I pomise you, I give you anyting you want, I do anyting -
Juss anyting you want. You juss ask... So... Whatchu want?" he says, trying to sound experienced and worldly, which he hopes will impress her.
A thoughtful silence follows and he waits patiently and eagerly for her request. She eventually shyly whispers back, "I want to try something I have heard about from other girls... Numbaa 69."
More thoughtful silence, this time from him.
Eventually, in a puzzled tone he asks her.
"You want... Garlic Chicken with steam vegetable?"

December 6th

Two cowboys are sitting swapping sex stories.
'What's your favourite position?' asks one
'The Rodeo' says the second
'I've not heard of that one'

'Well what you do is position your wife on all fours then mount her from behind. Reach around and gently caress her breasts and say 'Hey these feel just like your sisters' 'Then hold on and see how long before you fall off!!!'

December 7th

An elderly Italian man who lived on the outskirts of Rimini, Italy, went to the local church for confession.

When the priest slid open the panel in the confessional, the man said: 'Father ... During World War II, a beautiful Jewish woman from our neighbourhood knocked urgently on my door and asked me to hide her from the Nazis. So I hid her in my attic.'

The priest replied: 'That was a wonderful thing you did, and you have no need to confess that.'

'There is more to tell, Father... She started to repay me with sexual favours. This happened several times a week, and sometimes twice on Sundays.'

The priest said, 'That was a long time ago and by doing what you did, you placed the two of you in great danger. But two people under those circumstances can easily succumb to the weakness of the flesh. However, if you are truly sorry for your actions, you are indeed forgiven.'

'Thank you, Father. That's a great load off my mind. I do have one more question.'

'And what is that?' asked the priest.

'Should I tell her the war is over?'

December 8th
Two rednecks were walking along when they saw a dog licking its balls.
The first redneck said, "I wish I could do that."
The other redneck said, "You silly bugger, he would bite you."

December 9th
A little guy was sat at the bar when a thug walks over and smacks him in the face and says "that's Kung Fu from Japan".
A little later the thug smacks him again and says "That's Taekwondo from Korea".
The little guy leaves the bar.
A short time later he comes back into the bar, walks up to the thug and smacks him knocking him out cold and says to the barman, "When he wakes up, tell him that was a frigging shovel from B&Q!"

December 10th
A little girl is in line to see Santa. When it's her turn, she climbs up on Santa's lap. Santa asks, "What would you like Santa to bring you for Christmas?"
The little girl replies, "I want a Barbie and a G.I. Joe."
Santa looks at the little girl for a moment and says, "I thought Barbie comes with Ken."
"No," said the little girl. "She comes with G.I. Joe, she fakes it with Ken."

☺☺

December 11th

Couple in their nineties are both having problems remembering things. During a checkup, the doctor tells them that they're physically okay, but they might want to start writing things down to help them remember...

Later that night, while watching TV, the old man gets up from his chair. 'Want anything while I'm in the kitchen?' he asks.

'Will you get me a bowl of ice cream?'

"Sure"

'Don't you think you should write it down so you can remember it?' she asks.

'No, I can remember it.' "Well, I'd like some strawberries on top, too. Maybe you should write it down, so as not to forget it?"

"I can remember that. You want a bowl of ice cream with strawberries"

"I'd also like whipped cream. I'm certain you'll forget that, write it down?" she asks.

Irritated, he says, "I don't need to write it down, I can remember it! Ice cream with strawberries and whipped cream - I got it, for goodness sake!"

Then he toddles into the kitchen.

After about 20 minutes, the old man returns from the kitchen and hands his wife a plate of bacon and eggs.

She stares at the plate for a moment and says "Where's my toast?"

December 12th

Little 5 year old Daisy sees a group of workmen turn up next door to build a house.

She takes an interest and starts to talk to them.

The builders with hearts of gold adopt her as their site mascot.
After a week they present her with a pink hard hat and gloves, and a wage packet with £5 in.
"Goodness" says mommy smiling, "Are you working there next week?"
Daisy replies "I think so mummy, providing those bastards at Jewsons deliver the f***ing bricks on time.

December 13th

Two cowboys from Texas walk into a roadhouse to wash the trail dust from their throats. They stand at the bar drinking their beers and quietly talking about cattle prices. Suddenly a woman at a table behind them, who had been eating a sandwich, begins to cough. After a minute or so it becomes apparent that she is in real distress, and the cowboys turn to look at her.
"Kin ya swaller?" asks one of the cowboys.
No, the woman shakes her head.
"Kin ya breathe?" asks the other.
The woman, beginning to turn a bit blue, shakes her head no again.
The first cowboy walks over to her, lifts up the back of her skirt, yanks down her panties, and slowly runs his tongue from the back of her thigh up to the small of her back.
This shocks the woman into a violent spasm, the obstruction flies out of her mouth and she begins to breathe again.
The cowboy walks back over to the bar and takes a drink of his beer.
His partner says, "Ya know, I'd heard of that there Hind Lick Manoeuvre, but, I never seen anybody do it before."

December 14th

A petrol station owner in Dublin was trying to increase his sales. So, he put up a sign that read, 'Free Sex with Fill-Up. 'Soon Paddy pulled in, filled his tank and asked for his free sex. The owner told him to pick a number from 1 to 10. If he guessed correctly, he would get his free sex. Paddy guessed 8, and the proprietor said, 'You were close. The number was 7. Sorry. No sex this time.'

A week later, Paddy, along with his friend Mick, pulled in for another fill-up. Again he asked for his free sex. The proprietor again gave him the same story, and asked him to guess the correct number.

Paddy guessed 2 this time.

The proprietor said, 'Sorry, it was 3. You were close, but no free sex this time.'

As they were driving away, Mick said to Paddy, 'I think that game is rigged and he doesn't really give away free sex.

'Paddy replied, 'No it ain't, Mick. It's not rigged at all at all. My wife won twice last week.'

☺☺

December 15th

God said, 'Adam, I want you to do something for me.'
Adam said, 'Gladly, Lord, what do you want me to do?'
God said, 'Go down into that valley.'
Adam said, 'What's a valley?'
God explained it to Him. Then God said, 'Cross the river.'
Adam said, 'What's a river?'
God explained that to him, and then said, 'Go over to the hill....'

Adam said, 'What is a hill?'

So, God explained to Adam what a hill was.

He told Adam, 'On the other side of the hill you will find a cave.'

Adam said, 'What's a cave?'

After God explained, He said, 'In the cave you will find a woman.'

Adam said, 'What's a woman?'

So God explained that to him, too.

Then, God said, 'I want you to reproduce.'

Adam said, 'How do I do that?'

God first said (under his breath), 'Geez.....'

And then, just like everything else, God explained that to Adam, as well.

So, Adam goes down into the valley, across the river, over the hill, into the cave, and finds the woman.

Then, in about five minutes, he was back.

God, His patience wearing thin, said angrily, 'What is it now?'

And Adam said....

*

*

(YOU'RE GOING TO LOVE THIS!!!!!!)

*

*

*

*

'What's a headache?

☺☺

December 16th

All the organs of the body were having a meeting, trying to decide who was the one in charge.

I should be in charge,' said the brain, 'Because I run all the body's systems, so without me nothing would happen.'

'I should be in charge,' said the blood , 'because I circulate oxygen all over so without me you'd all waste away.'

'I should be in charge,' said the stomach , 'because I process food and give all of you energy..'

'I should be in charge,' said the legs, 'because I carry the body wherever it needs to go.'

'I should be in charge,' said the eyes, 'Because I allow the body to see where it goes.'

'I should be in charge,' said the rectum, 'Because I'm responsible for waste removal.'

All the other body parts laughed at the rectum and insulted him, so in a huff, he shut down tight.

Within a few days,

the brain had a terrible headache,

the stomach was bloated,

the legs got wobbly,

the eyes got watery,

and the blood was toxic.

They all decided that the rectum should be the boss.

The Moral of the story?

The arsehole is usually the one in charge!

December 17th

Little Johnny had a cussing problem and his father was getting tired of it. He decided to ask his shrink what to do. The shrink said, "Since Christmas is coming up, you should ask Johnny what he wants Santa to bring him. If he cusses while he tells you his wish list, leave a pile of dog poop in place of the gift or gifts he requests."

Two days before Christmas, Johnny's father asked him what he wanted for Christmas. "I want a damn teddy-bear laying right beside me when I wake-up. When I go downstairs I want to see a damn train going around the damn tree. And when I go outside I want to see a damn bike leaning up against the damn garage."

Christmas morning, Little Johnny woke up and rolled over into a pile of dog poop. Confused, he walked down stairs and saw another pile under the tree. Scratching his head, he walked outside and saw a huge pile of dog poop by the garage.

When Johnny walked back inside with a curious look on his face, his dad smiled and asked, "What did Santa bring you this year?"

Johnny replied, "I think I got a dog but I can't find the son-of-a-bitch!"

December 18th

Chinese guy walks into record shop in the UK and asks for a Cliff Richard record that he has heard on the radio.

What is it called ask the assistant

"Tits and Fanny " says the Chinese guy

"Dont think so mate - Cliff has never released a record with that title - he is a good Christian. Maybe you could sing it, and I'll see if I know it."

"Tits and fanny, that we don't talk anymore....Tits and fanny......" Belts out the Chinese guy.

December 19th

An Australian, an Irishman and a Scouser are in a bar. They're staring at another man sitting on his own at a table in the corner. He's so familiar, and not recognising him is driving them mad.

They stare and stare, until suddenly the Irishman twigs: 'My God, it's Jesus!'

Sure enough, it is Jesus, nursing a pint.

Thrilled, they send him over a pint of Guinness, a pint of Fosters and a pint of bitter. Jesus accepts the drinks, smiles over at the three men, and drinks the pints slowly, one after another.

After he's finished the drinks, Jesus approaches the trio. He reaches for the hand of the Irishman and shakes it, thanking him for the Guinness.

When he lets go, the Irishman gives a cry of amazement: 'My God! The arthritis I've had for 30 years is gone. It's a miracle!'

Jesus then shakes the Aussie's hand, thanking him for the lager.

As he lets go, the man's eyes widen in shock.

'Strewth mate, the bad back I've had all my life is completely gone! It's A Miracle.'

Jesus then approaches the Scouser who says, 'Back off, mate, I'm on disability benefit.'

December 20th

A woman was in town on a shopping trip. She began her day finding the most perfect shoes in the first shop and a beautiful dress on sale in the second. In the third everything had just been reduced to a fiver when her mobile phone rang. It was a female doctor notifying her that her husband had just been in a terrible accident and was in critical condition and in the ICU. The woman told the doctor to inform her husband where she was and that she'd be there as soon as possible.

As she hung up she realized she was leaving what was shaping up to be her best day ever in the shops. She decided to get in a couple of more shops before heading to the hospital.

She ended up shopping the rest of the morning, finishing her trip with a cup of coffee and a beautiful cream slice complementary from the last shop. She was jubilant.

Then she remembered her husband. Feeling guilty, she dashed to the hospital. She saw the doctor in the corridor and asked about her husband's condition.

The lady doctor glared at her and shouted, `You went ahead and finished your shopping trip didn't you! I hope you're proud of yourself! While you were out for the past four hours enjoying yourself in town, your husband has been languishing in the Intensive Care Unit! It's just as well you went ahead and finished, because it will more than likely be the last shopping trip you ever take! For the rest of his life he will require round the clock care. And you'll now be his carer!'

The woman was feeling so guilty she broke down and sobbed...........

The lady doctor then chuckled and said, 'I'm just pulling your leg.

He's dead. What did you buy?'

December 21st

After a long night of making love, the guy notices a photo of another man, on the woman's table by the bed. He begins to worry.

"Is this your husband?" he nervously asks.

"No, silly," she replies, snuggling up to him.

"Your boyfriend, then?" he continues.

"No, not at all," she says, nibbling away at his ear.

"Is it your dad or your brother?" He inquires, hoping to be reassured.

"No, no, no! You are so sexy when you're jealous!" she answers.

"Well, who in the hell is he, then?" he demands!!!!

She whispers in his ear "That's me before the surgery."

December 22nd

A blonde heard that milk baths would make her beautiful. She left a note for her milkman to leave 25 gallons of milk. When the milkman read the note, he felt there must be a mistake. He thought she probably meant 2.5 gallons. So he knocked on the door to clarify the point.

The blonde came to the door and the milkman said, "I found your note asking me to leave 25 gallons of milk. Did you mean 2.5 gallons?"

The blonde said, "I want 25 gallons. I'm going to fill my bathtub up with milk and take a milk bath so I can look young and beautiful again."

The milkman asked, "Do you want it pasteurised?"

The blonde said, "No, just up to my boobs. I can splash it on my eyes."

December 23rd

A couple returned from their honeymoon and it's obvious to everyone that they are not talking to each other.

The groom's best man takes him aside and asks what is wrong.

"Well," replied the man "when we had finished making love on the first night, as I got up to go to the bathroom I put a £50 bill on the pillow without thinking."

"Oh, you shouldn't worry about that too much," said his friend. "I'm sure your wife will get over it soon enough - she can't expect you to have been saving yourself all these years!"

The groom nodded gently and said, "I don't know if I can get over this though. She gave me £20 change!"

December 24th

Santa Claus, like all pilots, gets regular visits from the Federal Aviation Administration, and it was shortly before Christmas when the FAA examiner arrived.

In preparation, Santa had the elves wash the sled and bathe all the reindeer. Santa got his logbook out and made sure all his paperwork was in order.

The examiner walked slowly around the sled. He checked the reindeer harnesses, the landing gear, and Rudolf's nose. He painstakingly reviewed Santa's weight and balance calculations for the sled's enormous payload.

Finally, they were ready for the check ride. Santa got in, fastened his seatbelt and shoulder harness, and checked the compass. Then the examiner hopped in carrying, to Santa's surprise, a shotgun.

"What's that for?" asked Santa incredulously.

The examiner winked and said, "I'm not supposed to tell you this, but you're gonna lose an engine on takeoff."

☺☺

December 25th
Q. Why is Santa always happy?

A. Because he knows where all the bad girls live.

☺☺

This past Sunday, I was out on a pre-Christmas get together with friends. I had a few cocktails, followed by several glasses of wine. Despite my jolliness, I still had the sense to know that I was over the
limit. That's when I decided to do what I have never done before: I took a taxi home. Sure enough, there was a police road block on the road home but, since it was a taxi, they waved it past and I arrived home safely without incident.
This was both a great relief and a surprise because I had never driven a taxi before. I don't even know where I got it from and, now that it is in my garage, I don't know what to do with it.

☺☺

There were 3 guys who died on Christmas Eve & went to heaven. St. Peter at the gate said since you all died on Christmas Eve you have all got to show me something that represents Christmas.
First guy puts his hand in his pocket & pulled out a lighter, lights it and said "Candle".

St. Peter said there are candles for Christmas go in.
Second guy pulls out a set of keys & shakes them, saying bells.
St. Peter said there are bells for Christmas go in.
The third guys' pockets were turned inside out.
"Well" St. Peter said.
The guy puts his hand in his coat pocket & pulls out a pair of woman's panties
St. Peter said now what do they have to do with Christmas?
The guy said "Oh theses are Carols."

December 26th

My sister realised that our dog (a Schnauzer) was getting progressively deaf, so she took it to the vets. The vet found that the problem was hair growing in the dog's ears. He trimmed the hair and cleaned both ears, and the dog's hearing improved 100% back to normal. The vet then advised Joyce that, to keep this hair growth from recurring, she should buy some "Nair" hair remover and rub it in the dog's ears once a month.

Joyce went to the chemists and bought some "Nair" hair remover. As she was paying, the chemist said, "If you're going to use this under your arms, don't use any deodorant for a few days."

Joyce said, "I'm not using it under my arms."

The chemist said, "OK, if you're using it on your legs, doesn't use body lotion for a couple of days."

Joyce replied, "I'm not using it on my legs either............... If you must know, I'll be using it on my Schnauzer."

The chemists said, "Well, don't ride your bike for about a week."

☺☺

December 27th

A married man thought he would give his wife a birthday surprise by buying her a bra.

He entered a ladies shop rather intimidated, but the girls took charge to help him.

"What colour?" they asked. He settled for white.

"How much does it cost?" he asked. "Twenty dollars."

"Very good," he thought.

All that remained was the size, but he hadn't the faintest idea.

"Now sir, are they the size a pair of melons? Coconuts? Grapefruits? Oranges?"

"No," he said, "nothing like that."

"Come on, sir, think. There must be something your wife's bust resembles."

He thought long and hard and then looked up and said, "Have you ever seen a Spaniel's ears?"

December 28th

An Arab Sheik was admitted to St Vincents Hospital for heart surgery, but prior to the surgery the doctors needed to store his blood in case the need arose.

As the gentleman had a rare type of blood, it couldn't be found locally, so, the call went out to all the states.

Finally a Scot was located who had a similar blood type. The Scot willingly donated his blood for the Arab.

After the surgery, the Arab sent the Scotsman as appreciation for giving his blood, a new BMW, Diamonds & US dollars.

A couple of days later, once again, the Arab had to go through a corrective surgery.

His doctor telephoned the Scotsman who was more than happy to donate his blood again.

After the second surgery, the Arab sent the Scotsman a thank-you card & a jar of sweets.

The Scotsman was shocked that the Arab this time did not reciprocate his kind gesture as he had anticipated.

He phoned the Arab & asked him: "I thought you would be generous again, that you would give me a BMW, diamonds & money... But you only gave me a thank-you card & a jar of candies".

To this the Arab replied: "Aye, but I now have Scottish blood in my veins".

December 29th

A crusty old biker out on a long summer ride in the country pulled up to a tavern in the middle of nowhere, parked his bike, and walked inside. As he passed through the swinging doors, he saw a sign hanging over the bar:
COLD BEER: $2.00
HAMBURGER: $2.25
CHEESEBURGER: $2.50
CHICKEN SANDWICH: $3.50
HAND JOB: $50.00
Checking his wallet to be sure he had the necessary payment, the old biker walked up to the bar and beckoned to the exceptionally attractive female bartender who was serving drinks to a couple of sun-wrinkled farmers.

She glided down behind the bar to the old biker. "Yes?" she inquired with a wide, knowing smile, "may I help you?"

The old biker leaned over the bar. "I was wondering young lady," he whispered, "are you the one who gives the hand-jobs?"

She looks into his eyes with that wide smile and purred, "Why yes. Yes, I sure am."

The old biker leaned closer, and into her left ear whispers softly, "Well, wash your hands real good, `cause I want me a cheeseburger."

December 30th

An old cowboy sat down at the Starbucks counter and ordered a cup of coffee. As he sat sipping it, a young woman sat down next to him.

She turned to the cowboy and asked, "Are you a real cowboy?"

He replied, "Well, I've spent my whole life breaking colts, working cows, going to rodeos, fixing fences, pulling calves, bailing hay, doctoring calves, cleaning my barn, fixing flats, working on tractors, and feeding my dogs... so I guess I'm a cowboy."

She said, "I'm a lesbian. I spend my whole day thinking about naked women. As soon as I get up in the morning, I think about naked women. When I shower, I think about naked women. When I watch television, I think about naked women. It seems like everything makes me think of naked women."

The two sat sipping in silence.

A little while later, a man sat down on the other side of the old cowboy and asked, "Are you a real cowboy?"

He replied, "I always thought I was, but I just found out I'm really a lesbian!"

☺☺

December 31ˢᵗ

A woman accompanied her husband to the doctor's. After his check-up, the doctor called the wife into his office alone. He said, "Your husband is suffering from a very severe disease, combined with horrible stress. If you don't do the following, your husband will surely die.
Each morning, fix him a healthy breakfast. Be pleasant, and make sure he is in a good mood, don't burden him with chores, as this could further his stress. Try to relax your husband in the evening by wearing lingerie and giving him plenty of back rubs. Encourage him to watch some type of sport event on television. And most importantly, make love with your husband several times a week and satisfy his every whim. If you can do this for the next 9 months to a year, I think your husband will regain his health."
On the way home, the husband asked his wife, "What did the doctor say?"
"You're going to die," she replied.

'You might be an autism parent when you suddenly realise that you have forgotten yourself and the reason for the puzzled looks is that you have been speaking in keywords preceded by "listening".

Guilty as charged! We were out with friends last year and unbeknown to me I said 'Listening Kevin' before I spoke and our friends picked up on it. Of course it became a joke and everyone started saying it!

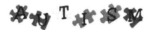

'You might be an autism parent when this year's Xmas presents are the same as last years and the year before, and anything different or a surprise is handed straight back with a 'no thank you.'

I have to buy books that are out of production on ebay that we have maybe seven or eight times and keep a stock of in the wardrobe for birthdays and Christmases because that is what she wants. We have all her DVD's duplicated in case we can't get hold of one if they ever break, and still have all the videos from before DVD's were invented because she will not let us throw them away.

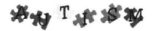

'You might be an autism parent when your child is a pro at stopping a video on the same exact syllable 63 times in a row'

People marvel at Rachel's ability to do this, she does it with tapes, videos and DVD's, playing and rewinding them to exactly the same spot over and over and over without even looking at them. You do become oblivious to it and it is only when visitors comment that your brain clicks in and realises what is happening. Other people say leave it and let's see what happens but there is no chance of that ever happening!

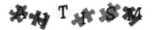

'You know you are the parent of an autistic child when you have said "I love you" a million times and waited for 20 years to hear it back.'

This is actually fact for me! Rachel first said 'I love you' one night when I put her to bed and she has only ever said it once more since, but one thing I can say is I have never been loved quite this deeply or unconditionally before. It is a pure love with no grudges, ever.

WHY?

Because people on the autistic spectrum rarely lie, the truth is the truth, they don't judge people, they aren't tied to social expectations. What you see is what you get. There are no hidden agendas, they are less materialistic and have fantastic memories.

Autistic people are awesome!

If you don't already know someone with autism
– the chances are you soon will!

Made in the USA
Charleston, SC
18 February 2015